ALSO BY JOSEPH STONE

WRITING AS G. A. DAZIO

SLAVE

THE GHOST OF CAMBRIA

BOOK TWO

JOSEPH STONE

SILVER LION
PUBLISHING

EDITOR: Jerrica McDowell

COVER ART: Daqri Bernardo, Covers By Combs

DEDICATION

For Elaine Chaney,
a cherished friend and advocate who insisted I
avoid anything to do with Ouija boards,

and

For Paula McCambridge,
a remarkable woman who placed
her hands upon the Ouija indicator with me.

EPIGRAPH

What looked like morning
  was the beginning of endless night.

— WILLIAM PETER BLATTY, *THE EXORCIST*

CHAPTER ONE

Kristen Cole sat at a patio table on her home's rear deck, under a large canvas umbrella and surrounded by sheriff officers. With her red hair pulled back into a haphazard bun, Kristen wore the simple black tank-top and jeans she'd dressed in for the previous day's wine-tasting date in Paso Robles. The woman felt numb, in dire need of coffee to focus her thoughts. But the numbness was the only respite from the confused horror she'd experienced those morning hours. Kristen had discovered her lover, Ryan Hoffman, dead on her bathroom floor.

"What time was that?" a sheriff asked.

Kristen couldn't remember the man's name, which he'd given her only moments earlier. There wasn't room for anything else in her mind, the terrifying images and sounds occluded the present as they ran repeatedly.

"I found him around four o'clock," Kristen answered. "I woke up and went to use the bathroom. Then I called you moments after."

"And when was the last time you'd seen him before that moment?" said the officer.

"He went to use the bathroom before we went to bed. That was about seven-thirty. We were about to…" Kristen stopped, uncertain of what to say.

"To have intimate relations?" the officer offered.

"Yes," Kristen answered. "We were both very drunk. Ryan was having trouble walking, and when he finally got in the bathroom, I heard him fall. I just laughed because it seemed so funny at the time. Then I waited for him in bed and eventually passed out, from the drink, I mean."

But then Kristen had woken up at three-fifteen, the alarm clock on her bedside table the only source of light in the room. Before she could understand what had happened, Kristen felt Ryan's hands on her body, his mouth on her sex. He'd made love to her in the dark, bringing her to climax. And when they finished, Ryan told Kristen he loved her and wanted her to stay with him.

"So, you expect the fall you heard was when Mister Hoffman had his accident?" the sheriff asked.

Kristen hadn't needed a forensics expert to tell her that the pool of blood under Ryan's head, dried around the edges, was hours old. There was no way he could've made love to her and then died moments before she discovered him on the bathroom floor.

"It must have been," Kristen answered as she stared at the table with a lifeless gaze.

There wasn't a doubt in her mind. Alcohol or not, Kristen had not imagined half-an-hour of sexual inter-course in the dark of her bedroom. Her mind had been awake, conscious of each sensation. Kristen remembered the invasions of his tongue and cock; the hardness of his body pressed against hers; his teeth nibbling on her earlobe; his hot breath as he lovingly whispered to her.

It wasn't Ryan who had made love to Kristen that morning. It was the other man, the one with steel-blue eyes set under a dark brow who had visited Kristen in her dreams. He had made love to Kristen while she dreamt of being with other men. And as Kristen's mind had woken, his sex still firm within her, the handsome man had vanished before her very eyes. Kristen had suffered in agony each time, realizing that she was a victim to some sort of delusion brought on by her grief.

But she knew better now—the man was by no means a delusion. He was a ghost.

TONY SPENT a good deal of the previous evening thinking about the way he'd been dumped for the clown who'd picked Kristen up yesterday. He knew it was unreasonable of him to add to the situation. In the end, it didn't matter how Tony felt about Kristen or what he wanted from her. At best, he was a friend with benefits. Not even a friend, if Tony was honest with himself. Kristen was his boss, and everything else was nothing more than his fantasy.

If Tony hadn't taken the dog to keep overnight, he would have hit up a bar and found someone to make himself feel better about the situation. Instead, he'd taken the Husky on a five-mile run that she loved. Tony let her hog the bed, and she was perfectly happy to cuddle into a deep sleep with her new human, even if he was, in the end, only pretending.

This morning, Penny sat beside Tony on the passenger side of his truck, her head extended through the open window to watch the world as they drove past it. When they pulled onto their final turn shortly before eight o'clock, paramedics and fire trucks confronted them with red emergency lights that rotated from all around. Kristen's driveway was chock full of sheriff vehicles. The animated scene flashed in their eyes as Tony and Penny passed by, the established perimeter of implied authority prompting them to drive on.

Tony pulled in to park a couple of homes down the road. Though Penny's excitement to be home was unmistakable, Tony left her locked inside the truck cabin, cracking the windows a few inches open.

The young man made his way down the street apprehensively to Kristen's house, where two neighbors stood just outside black and yellow 'Do Not Cross' tape. They spoke with an officer guarding the erected perimeter who appeared disinterested in their questions. When the officer saw Tony approach, she instantly turned to appraise him.

"Sir, I will need you to stand back," she said with polite aggression.

"Officer, is everything alright?" he asked. "I'm working on this house for Kristen Cole."

"What's your name?" the sheriff asked.

"Tony De Luca. I am a contractor."

The officer reached for a small black broach attached by a heavy wire to the two-way radio on her belt. Turning, she mumbled into the receiver, and in moments a second sheriff emerged from the house to make his way down the slope of the front lawn. After a nod from his partner, the officer gestured for Tony to step to the side where they could speak privately.

"Good morning, sir, I'm Sheriff Comstock. You're Tony De Luca?" the officer verified.

"Yes, sir," said Tony. "I'm working here for Ms. Cole on the refurbishment of the house. What's happened?"

In the distance, Tony saw that two paramedics were balancing a stretcher down the steps of the front porch.

On the apparatus appeared to be a body covered by a white sheet.

"Jesus Christ! Is she dead?" the young man panicked.

"Ms. Cole is inside, and she isn't hurt," the officer confirmed.

"May I see her?" asked Tony as an urgent fear took over his expression.

"I'm sorry, I can't let you in, but I wanted to ask you a couple of questions," the very calm man answered Tony. "When were you last here?"

"I left yesterday around six--when I finished for the day," the young man answered promptly.

"And when was the last time you spoke with Ms. Cole?"

"I received a phone call from her just a few minutes before I left," said Tony. "Kristen called to let me know she was coming home later than she'd planned and asked if I would leave the lights on for her before I locked up."

From his peripheral vision, Tony saw a black Tesla sports car parked on the street in front of the house. It was blocked in by the emergency vehicles. Tony finally realized who the paramedics lifted into the ambulance.

"Is it the man she was on a date with? His name is Ryan. That's his car," said Tony pointing to the Tesla.

The sheriff didn't take his eyes from Tony.

"Would you be able to give a statement this morning at the sheriff's station in San Luis Obispo?" asked the officer. "The detective in charge will likely have questions for you."

"I guess," said Tony, unsure of what he had been asked. "I have Kristen's dog with me. She's in my truck, just there," and he pointed behind him.

"We can't let the animal in, either. You'll need to keep

the animal with you or find someone else to take it off your hands for now," the officer confirmed.

He pulled out a business card with the name of the police station and address.

"If you can stop by in about an hour, we would appreciate it," the officer added.

"Yeah, sure," said Tony examining the card as he received it.

He gave the scene a long look before turning back to his truck. Opening the vehicle door, Penelope fidgeted with anticipation at the prospect of being let out, but Tony signaled for her to back up on the bench seat so he could enter. With the driver's door closed behind him, Tony gave Penny attention with one hand as he examined the card in the other.

San Luis Obispo County Sheriff's Office
1585 Kansas Avenue
San Luis Obispo, CA 93405

Tony's immediate notion of Ryan being dead was silent gratitude, but he was upset with himself for wishing such a thing upon someone who didn't deserve his ire. The confusion of it all unsettled Tony, and he started the motor.

"Let's go for a little trip," he said sweetly to the Husky, who was instantly happy when he rolled her window down. The truck pulled forward into the lane, and the cool wind swept again through her fur.

CHAPTER TWO

Detective Laura Rodrigo closed the door to her office to escape the noise of the sheriff's station. She needed a moment to collect her thoughts before her scheduled meeting with the station's forensics analyst began. Forefront on the detective's mind was how she'd failed to answer the call this morning, a failure that would likely have repercussions from her peers and subordinates, rather than her supervisor, the field operations chief. Rodrigo had gone to bed in the middle of an argument, slept poorly, and nothing could pry her eyes open this morning when the call came in at five o'clock. It was a failure others would have been reprimanded for, but it had more significant consequences for the detective due to the position of authority she assumed. Rodrigo needed the people around her to do their best, and any reason for them to fall short of it placed the function of the office at risk.

The dark wood-covered walls of her office offered a relief from the uniform off-white surfaces throughout the rest of the San Luis Obispo County Sheriff's Office. Rodrigo closed her eyes and focused on her breathing, attempting to reach a meditative state. It was a method the detective employed before each interview, an invaluable tool for removing any stimulus that might distract from her observations of a suspect.

Rodrigo's office had been ordered to a house in Cambria when a paramedics call had flagged their system. A thirty-six-year-old man, Ryan Hoffman, had been reported dead due to an accidental fall. Hoffman had fatally struck his head against the edge of a bathtub. However, another man, the home's owner, Richard Cole, had been found dead under similar circumstances barely a month earlier.

"Las Vegas offers better odds," Rodrigo whispered to herself.

She had not discovered a motive, but only one of the potential suspects had yet been interviewed, albeit shortly on the scene. Kristen Cole had reported Hoffman's death early that morning. The pair were lovers, and Hoffman had spent the night with her. She was the daughter of Richard Cole—the man found dead for similar reasons. The second suspect, Tony De Luca, was the only other person with regular access to the home. Before Rodrigo would interview either, she would wait for the initial forensic report.

Rodrigo felt the tension in her shoulders abate just as her focus became sharp. The achievement ended after a knock came from the door.

"Come in," the detective answered heavily.

"Good morning, ma'am," said Ivan Llanda, the station's forensic analyst.

The lean man wore a black station polo shirt tucked neatly into his khaki pants. He closed the door behind him and sat down without being asked, the pair's routine already well-established. In his hands, he held a report folder, which he opened to begin his review.

"What have you got for me?" asked Rodrigo calmly, her eyes on him.

"We had luck with the print analysis," Llanda began. "Of the three we pulled in the bedroom that weren't latent, two have already come back. The first belongs to the deceased, Ryan Hoffman, who was retired military. The second is from Kristen Cole, who is registered in the system as a clinical psychologist working in San Diego."

"The third didn't come back as the father's?" asked Rodrigo. "He was living in the room four weeks ago. He died in the bathroom."

"No, we didn't find his prints in the bathroom," Llanda continued. "I expect the space was professionally cleaned after he died. But we did find his prints on the bedframe and bedroom doors, as well as the unidentified prints."

"Probably from the contractor working on the remodel," asserted Rodrigo. *Why would he touch the bed*, she wondered, envisioning two possible scenarios. "He's scheduled to be here in ten minutes."

"His prints were on the bedroom door and bedframe, but not in the bathroom," Llanda clarified.

Rodrigo exhaled sharply, her breath breaking through her calmness.

"That doesn't do much for us," she said with a color of impatience.

"Hoffman died sometime between seven and nine o'clock yesterday evening," answered Llanda, ignoring the detective's tone.

"Which matches Cole's assertion," Rodrigo offered. "So why are we even bothering with this?"

"Because Richard Cole was found in the same bathroom with the same fatal injury," said Llanda, and he lifted his gaze from the report as he handed it to Rodrigo.

"Fine," conceded Rodrigo, "I'm no apologist for coincidences either. But I have two potential suspects for Hoffman's death, which you've more or less told me was an accident. Neither holds up for Richard Cole's death, which was also declared an accident. We can likely prove the daughter was in San Diego at the time of her father's death. That leaves us the contractor, who we have no forensic evidence was ever in the bathroom. As well as Cole's insistence that she and Hoffman were alone all night."

"That hardly makes it impossible," countered Llanda.

"No," Rodrigo shook her head, "but what would cause a young man to kill someone he didn't know? What would then cause the contractor to go to work for his daughter in the same house, then kill her boyfriend the same way he killed her father?"

Llanda didn't respond.

"The alternative you're offering me is that Kristen Cole didn't kill her father, but killed her boyfriend and made it appear identical to how her father died? The possible motivation being…?"

Llanda remained silent.

"So," the detective nodded, "there's not much for us to go on. Aside from our agreement that this is an unlikely coincidence."

A knock came from the door, and Rodrigo gestured through her office's glass wall for the young man standing outside to enter.

"Kristen Cole is here for an interview," said the man. "I've placed her in Room A for you."

"Thank you," Rodrigo answered without looking up, her eyes locked on her wristwatch as she rose.

The detective moved into the hallway outside her office, leaving the forensic analyst where he sat without a word of dismissal, and strode through the station to the interview rooms. The tall woman's stride was steady and formidable, and she passed through the building without drawing conversation from the people who looked up to notice her.

Arriving at Room A, Rodrigo glanced through the small door window to observe Kristen Cole for a moment before opening the door and stepping into the unattractive eight-by-seven space. A cup of coffee sat in front of the doctor on the small round office table. The sound of Rodrigo entering drew Cole's attention at once.

"Hello, Doctor Cole," said Rodrigo with a condoling half-smile and conciliatory tone. "Thank you for coming in this morning. I know this is probably the last thing you want to be doing, but it's imperative we do this while the event is still fresh in your mind."

"I understand," said Kristen with tired red eyes.

"I would like to record this interview for our files. However, if you don't wish me to, you have the right to refuse. Also, if you would like someone here with you, they are welcome to join us."

"I'm fine if you record the interview, and there's no one to join me," Kristen answered.

"Very good, just give me a moment," said Rodrigo.

The detective turned to a small panel in the wall where a television monitor was lit, displaying Kristen and a sign on the wall behind her stating the day's date. After pressing a button, the screen flashed the symbol for Record, and Rodrigo closed the panel before sitting down across from the interviewee.

"Today is September eighteenth, twenty-nineteen," she began, "and this interview is being recorded in Interview

Room A of the San Luis Obispo Sheriff's Office. The interviewer is Detective Laura Rodrigo, employed by the same office. The interviewee is Doctor Kristen Cole of fifty-eight-zero-five Friars Road, apartment twenty-four-fifteen in San Diego, California. Doctor Cole has waived her right to prevent this interview from being recorded and has not asked for a third party to join her.

"Doctor Cole," Rodrigo looked up, "is that all correct?"

"Yes, it is," Kristen answered.

"Very well, let's begin."

CHAPTER THREE

The interview began with a formal review of the information the doctor had already provided. Kristen had last seen Ryan Hoffman as he entered the master bathroom around seven-thirty yesterday evening. Kristen heard Hoffman fall to the floor, and laughed off the accident, attributing it to his intoxication. Kristen fell asleep as she waited for him to rejoin her in the bedroom. Kristen woke and discovered Hoffman's body in the bathroom shortly before four o'clock a.m.

Kristen confirmed each point both verbally and with a nod before Rodrigo sat back in her seat and began the meat of the interview.

"Are you employed in San Diego?" asked Rodrigo.

"Yes. I work for Scripps Medical Center in La Jolla as a clinical psychologist," Kristen answered, adding the address.

"And you're a doctor of psychology?" the detective confirmed.

"I have a doctorate from the University of California, San Diego," Kristen nodded.

"Why were you in Cambria yesterday?" asked the woman.

"I've been here for three weeks now," said Kristen. "I arrived after my father passed away at the end of August. I've stayed in town to prepare his house, my parent's house, for sale."

"Will you remain in Cambria until the remodel is complete, or you sell the house, or...?" Rodrigo asked.

"I had planned on leaving this week. We've had a couple of bumps along the way, but I hired a contractor to oversee the renovations for me so I could return to work in San Diego," Kristen clarified.

"You mentioned the contractor to Sheriff Pomeroy this morning. What is the man's name again?"

"Tony De Luca," said Kristen.

"How did you meet Mister De Luca?"

"He had met with my father about renovating the house. Then after my dad passed, I hired Tony to complete the work they had planned together."

Rodrigo paused, her eyes remaining fixed on Kristen.

"How long has Mister De Luca been working in the house?" she continued.

"The past two and a half weeks, near about," said Kristen

"He was going to manage the repairs for you, and you were planning to entrust the house to him after you returned south?" Rodrigo asked.

"Correct," confirmed Kristen.

"Does Mister De Luca have a key to the house?" the detective added.

"Yes, he has the key," said Kristen. "He's been letting himself in each morning—he starts his day very early. He also locks up on the way out if I'm not in the house before he leaves. But he's always on site when other construction workers are there."

"But Mister De Luca wasn't there when you and Mister Hoffman came home from your date?" Rodrigo asked.

"No. Our date ran long, and Tony locked up the house before he left for the day."

"Sheriff Comstock showed you a note—I apologize for not having it with me," said the detective. "I believe Mister De Luca wrote it to you. The one we found it on the first floor. Do you remember it?"

"Yes, he had written to let me know he was taking Penelope with him," answered Kristen.

"Penelope is your dog?" the woman asked.

"Yes," said Kristen with a nod.

"The note said the dog was restless and that he was taking her for a run?" the detective asked with a slight frown, the first bit of emotion she had displayed since they began.

"I just adopted the dog last week, and because of her young age and breed, Penelope requires a lot of exercise, or she can become a handful. Tony grew up with the breed—she's a Siberian Husky—so he's been a godsend in helping her to adjust to her new environment. He's helped us adjust to each other, to be honest. I realize it must seem weird for a contractor to take off with his employer's dog, but I assure you Tony was just acting kindly. I had called him to say I was running late during my date, and he probably realized that Penelope wouldn't get the walk she needed."

"But he kept her overnight instead of bringing the dog home after the run?" inquired Rodrigo.

"Tony knew I was out on a date with Ryan," she answered, pursing her lips with a shrug. "He probably didn't want to bother us. Also, he gets along well with the dog. I think Penelope probably likes him more than she likes me. ...I don't mean to sound jealous." Kristen sniffed at her statement as if it seemed tragically humorous. "But I was grateful I didn't have to interrupt our date to walk her when Ryan and I got home."

"Why were you and Mister Hoffman late coming home?"

"He took me to Paso Robles to go wine tasting. We stopped at one winery after the next, and by the time we headed back, we hit the afternoon traffic."

"Mister Hoffman drove?"

"Yes, he did."

"He was intoxicated?"

"Well, he drove us out to the area, but his car did the driving for the rest of the day. He has one of those Tesla cars that drives itself. It even parks itself. It's quite remarkable."

Kristen's eyes faltered, realizing she had spoken of Ryan as if he were still alive.

"I'm sorry. I guess I should say he had the car," Kristen added, smiling weakly to stave off more tears.

"Not at all," said Rodrigo, and she let Kristen collect herself. "Before I continue, I need to let you know that it's still illegal to operate a car while you're intoxicated, even if the car is driving itself. I understand that you were a passenger, but you seemed to dismiss it just then, and I want to make certain you understand. ...In case you find yourself driving one in the future."

"I didn't realize that," winced Kristen.

"It's not one-hundred percent yet, the technology that operates them. But even when it is—if the autopilot disengages for any reason, the driver needs to be able to take over."

"I see. I guess that makes sense."

Detective Rodrigo nodded and returned to the interview.

"You mentioned that you were jealous of your pet's relationship with Mister De Luca…"

"I don't know why I said that," Kristen winced. "I was just making a nervous joke."

Rodrigo nodded.

"Do you think Mister De Luca was jealous of you and Mister Hoffman for any reason?"

Kristen froze as the detective's direction became clear.

"Tony's a sweet guy, but ours is a professional relationship," Kristen answered, adrenaline coursing through her veins. "He's almost a decade younger than me. I'm not saying it's impossible that he might be jealous of Ryan. Frankly, many men would be. Ryan was unusually accomplished in his career—he seemed to be very well off. Last week he took me to a charity party where he donated millions of dollars to help school children."

Rodrigo raised her brows in surprise.

"I'm not prone to jealousy myself," added Kristen, "but if I was going to pick someone to envy…"

Kirsten shrugged, attempting to sell the lie. She didn't want to lie; it wasn't in her nature. Kristen thought lies were usually about the dumbest choice a person could make. But she was now terrified the detective would finger Tony for Ryan's death, and she didn't believe the young man was capable of such a thing.

"I tend to agree with you, which is why the thought occurred to me," Rodrigo offered. "Do you know if they ever spoke?"

"Once or twice," acknowledged Kristen. "I introduced them the first time Ryan picked me up for a date, and they spoke while Ryan was waiting for me to get ready to leave. Nothing more that I know of."

"Doctor Cole, I'll be honest with you, it surprises me that you seem so unconcerned about Mister De Luca," Rodrigo declared gently, sitting back in her chair. "Your father and Mister Hoffman both died in what seems to be the same manner—in the same place, no less. And the only commonalities linking them are Mister De Luca and yourself. Am I mistaken?"

Kristen's heart sank upon hearing the detective's words.

"It surprises me that you think a twenty-four-year-old would have any reason to kill a sixty-eight-year-old he barely knew," Kristen countered. "I'm sure you can imagine I'm well-versed in the indicators of anti-social and psychopathic personality traits. I can assure you that Tony exhibits none of them. I agree that jealousy could be a motivator in such a hypothetical crime between men. But if you ever saw this kid, you might wonder who was more jealous of whom. I encourage you to interview him —I'm certain you'll find nothing there."

Rodrigo blinked as if she'd been stopped in her line of thought, but only for a moment.

"Doctor Cole, we don't much care for coincidences in this office," the detective offered bluntly.

"Me either," Kristen exhaled. "In my work, only a few red flags are brighter. But I guarantee you that I didn't kill my father, and I sure as hell didn't kill my millionaire boyfriend with whom I'd only been on four dates. So, if all we have to go on is Tony, then I have no reason to believe this wasn't an unfortunate coincidence. As much as the notion unsettles me, I have to admit that coincidences do exist."

"Very well, I'm going to interview Mister De Luca next," said the detective dismissively, and she closed her notebook abruptly to rise from her chair.

Moving to the A/V panel, Rodrigo stopped the video recording.

"The department will contact you with a status on our investigation. For now, I am going to ask you to stay out of the master bedroom in your house."

"I see," said Kristen.

Rodrigo turned to walk out of the little room without another word.

CHAPTER FOUR

Detective Rodrigo didn't bother to ask if Tony De Luca had arrived. She turned down the corridor to Rooms B and C to let her eyes determine the answer. The lights weren't on in the first room as Rodrigo passed, but the detective could see the glow coming from Room C.

Glancing in the small door window, she saw him. De Luca was a young man with tousled brown hair that lightly grazed the top of his eyebrows. His was an Italian name with features to match, but Rodrigo thought she saw something else in his eyes. His skin was tanned such that she couldn't be sure if its base were Mediterranean olive or light Aztec. The young man sat dressed in a simple white crew-neck t-shirt, his arms covered in dark tattoos, the shades of black ink extending down to his hardly muscled forearms. He owned a handsome face, but the boy was so physically fit that people probably never noticed it in passing. The detective was not sexually attracted to men, but anyone could guess Mr. De Luca had turned more than a few heads in his time.

If anything, Cole's assertion that De Luca didn't fit a

jealous personality type didn't seem based on the doctor's imagination. More to the point, Rodrigo saw nothing in his eyes that indicated the presence of a predator. There was only light there, even in his anxiety—De Luca's bright brown eyes had yet to grow out of their boyish innocence.

From down the hall, the detective heard footsteps approach, and she turned her head to see the front desk officer approaching.

"That's Tony De Luca," he said rather loudly.

Rodrigo silently nodded to the man, then turned her eye back to see De Luca staring up at her through the glass. She smiled and took the handle to enter the small room.

"Good morning, Mister De Luca. I'm Detective Rodrigo," she said, extending her hand.

He stood awkwardly to receive her handshake. The man's palms were clammy. He was as nervous as he appeared—another indicator that she wasn't speaking to a predator. A serial murderer wouldn't be capable of such anxiety.

"Please," she gestured for De Luca to re-seat himself. "Thank you for coming in this morning. I wanted to ask you a few questions about your employer, Kristen Cole."

"Okay," Tony answered with a deep voice and firm nod.

"This is a formal interview, and we prefer to record it, but if you wish for us not to, that is your right," she said with concerned eyes.

"No, I understand—it's cool," replied De Luca.

"And if you would prefer a third person to be in the room with us while we speak, you are more than welcome to invite them," the detective added gently.

Her tone seemed to back-fire, and De Luca looked suspicious of the statement.

"Does that mean I need an attorney?" the young man eyed her with concern.

Rodrigo smiled brightly, at once certain of who she was dealing with. The detective took a seat so as not to tower over the man while she answered his question.

"Well, by law, I'm not permitted to instruct that you don't need an attorney," she offered. "But I can say that if you decide you want to consult one before we begin, that is with your right. If you want your best friend or a parent to sit here with you, that's okay too."

Rodrigo pursed her lips in a sly smile and shook her head almost imperceptibly to convey he didn't need assistance. It was a violation to suggest it, but she already knew De Luca wasn't guilty of murder. The detective didn't care to delay the interview and waste any more time on the young man's fears.

At the sight of her warm smile, De Luca visibly relaxed.

"No, that's cool. I'm good to go," he answered.

"Very well," said Rodrigo, and she rose to turn on the room's video recording device quickly, then returned to her chair.

"The sheriff who you spoke with at Doctor Cole's house this morning told me you guessed the body we removed from the house was Ryan Hoffman, is that correct?"

"Yes," he said. "Well, I saw his car parked in front. I guessed..."

"All right, I will confirm that it was, in fact, Mister Hoffman's body."

De Luca looked as if he were relieved by her confirmation.

"Did he have a heart attack or something?" the young man asked.

"I'm afraid that we can't discuss with you the cause of Mister Hoffman's death, but I also want to reaffirm with you that while we are recording, this must be a one-way interview. Do you understand? I'm the one who must ask the questions, and you must be the one who answers. If you have questions when we're finished, I will be happy to answer whatever I can."

"I'm sorry, I get it. Please," Tony nodded to her.

The detective could see the young man's manners were not subterfuge. He was perfectly sincere.

"That's quite all right," Rodrigo smiled warmly. "Why don't you start by telling me how you knew Mister Hoffman?"

"I didn't know him at all, really," he said, looking to the wall on his left. "He started dating Kristen a couple of weeks ago, and I spoke to him a little bit when he was at the house to visit her."

"What did you talk about?" she asked.

"Nothing, really," the young man shook his head. "He asked me how the renovations were coming along. I told him what I was working on at that moment. But I was on the job, and it wasn't much more than polite talking."

"Was he only at the house when Doctor Cole was at home?" the detective asked.

"Yeah, he only ever came by the house for her," he answered.

"Did you ever notice any problem they had with each other?" she asked.

"No," he shook his head. "Well, she was a bit annoyed with him sometimes."

"Annoyed?" asked Rodrigo, and she slightly cocked her head.

"I can't really be sure," he shrugged, "I only overheard

parts of what she said. But I think Kristen was annoyed when he would show up at the house uninvited."

"When was that?" she asked.

"A couple of times," said De Luca, "last week and yesterday morning. He showed up without calling ahead to ask her out on a date. I guess that was him being spontaneous? It seemed to bother her."

The young man raised his eyebrows and shrugged.

"But she got over it, I guess," he added. "She left with him each time."

"Did that bother you at all?" Rodrigo asked quietly.

The young man immediately scowled and shook his head, as if it weren't worth mentioning. The act revealed something she hadn't expected of De Luca since laying eyes upon him.

"Did you know Doctor Cole's father before he passed away?" she asked.

"Yes, old man Cole. He was a doctor too. Kristen followed in his footsteps, he told me. He was a super cool guy."

"When did you meet him?" asked Rodrigo.

"Like, maybe a week before he died," De Luca answered.

"Where did you meet him?" she asked when the young man didn't elaborate.

"Oh, at his house," he added. "I was in the neighborhood looking for work, and I saw him sitting on his front porch. He probably thought I was lost, but I was looking at the houses along the street to see if any of them looked like they needed work done. And, well, …have you seen it? She's got beautiful bones, but she needs more than a coat of paint."

"And you offered your services to Mister Cole, or, excuse me, Doctor Cole Senior?"

"Yeah," he nodded. "Richard was really nice and let me look inside the house. He didn't have money to do the job, not for what the house really needed. So, we talked about it, and I offered to do the work for free if he would let me work at my own pace and just pay for the materials that…"

"So, you didn't have any problems with the man?" she interrupted him.

"No, he was an excellent guy," said De Luca with a perplexed expression. "I only got to talk to him that one time for a couple of hours at the most."

"And how did you meet his daughter?" she pressed.

"Well, I came back to the house because Richard hadn't called me, and I really thought he was going to. He seemed excited about my offer. Anyhow, when I got there, she let me know he'd passed away."

"Did she tell you how her father had died?" Rodrigo eyed him.

"She said he fell while he was alone and died," De Luca told the detective. "He didn't show up for work and didn't call, so they contacted her, …and she contacted you guys."

"Did she say where he died in the house?" the detective cut in again.

"She only said it happened upstairs," Tony shrugged.

"Were you ever in Doctor Cole's bedroom?" the detective asked.

"Richard showed it to me," he nodded, misunderstanding the detective's question, "but I didn't spend much time in it. It was the only room that didn't need to renovate. The previous owner had redone the bathroom completely."

"How about after he passed. Did Kristen Cole ever ask you into her bedroom?" she asked.

De Luca flinched, his eyes swelling with concern. There it is, Rodrigo thought.

"Ah…" the young man paused.

"Have you ever had sexual relations with her?" asked Rodrigo with an emotionless, clinical expression.

De Luca fidgeted in his chair slightly, but the reaction was unmistakable. Rodrigo saw the tattoos on his arm more clearly. There were drawings of a forest. Was that a wolf, she wondered as the young man brought his hand up to scratch his scalp, exposing his inner bicep.

"I'd rather not discuss any of that," he said, looking down at the table.

"You don't have to if you'd rather not," Rodrigo conceded.

"It's just, we only hooked up a couple of times, but nothing came of it. She asked that we didn't talk about it because …it wasn't going to go anywhere and she didn't want it to get around, I guess. It was just …you know."

The bitch had two guys in two weeks and hardly knew either of them, Rodrigo thought, preventing a bemused expression from taking hold of her face. *I've finally turned into the old lady my mother promised I'd become.*

"I understand," she lifted her palm gently to relieve him of his need to explain further. "That's all I have, really."

The detective rose from her chair and turned off the recording unit.

"Did you have any questions before I let you go?"

"What happens now?" he asked, anxiety still present in his eyes.

"I doubt we'll need anything more from you, but I'll be in contact if I do," Rodrigo answered.

"Will I be able to go back to work on the house?" asked De Luca.

"For now, we've asked Doctor Cole to stay out of the master bedroom," she answered. "As for the construction work, that's a question for her to answer."

"Please don't tell Kristen I discussed the sex part with you," he implored quietly. "I think she'd be embarrassed."

Rodrigo couldn't help the incredulous expression that sat behind her smile.

"I wouldn't concern myself with that if I were you," she offered as kindly as she could. "But, off the record, I think you're sniffing up the wrong tree."

The detective nodded gently for De Luca to follow her out of the room and led him down the corridor.

"Check-out with the front desk, and you're good to go. Have a nice day," she offered and turned to her office.

It bothered the hell out of Rodrigo that Cole had lied to her about her relationship with De Luca. It was perfectly obvious why she had done so, but that didn't leave Rodrigo any less agitated. There was no reason for Cole to have murdered Hoffman, but any lie forced the detective to leave the door to that possibility cracked open.

Before she arrived at her office door, Llanda stepped into the corridor.

"Figure it out?" the analyst asked her.

"I didn't figure out how they both died in the bath-room, but I did figure out neither of our suspects did it," she answered with a hint of impatience.

"Dead end, then?" Llanda asked.

"I'll leave it pending for a few days," the detective clarified, "in case you turn up something else. But I'm done."

CHAPTER FIVE

Tony felt lighter as he walked through the sheriff's station parking lot towards his truck. The midday breeze swept through his hair, soothing Tony's nerves, and relaxing his stride. He gratefully felt each step settle the remaining adrenaline from his system.

The man couldn't believe he had confirmed the detective's question about how he and Kristen had hooked up. Tony should've said nothing, but he even told the woman how upset Kristen would be if the story got out. He was beyond irritated with himself and prayed his loose lips didn't get back to his boss.

Tony had thankfully managed not to bring up his conversation with Ryan at the gym. *At least I didn't have to fucking explain that,* he thought, shaking his head pathetically. At first, Tony didn't understand why the detective had asked him those questions, but he soon recognized she was looking for a reason to connect him with Ryan's death. It couldn't have been a heart attack, he realized. They think someone killed him, he mused, and he and I didn't get along.

Well, that wasn't right, not really. The two men had never fought. Though Tony would've liked to give the fucker a shot in the mouth. Anyone in that shower would say the two of them were just taking the piss out of each other, even if Ryan was the only one acting like a fucking asshole. They all probably thought the guy was funny.

Maybe she killed him? Perhaps the fucker got out of hand, and she fought back? The entire thing didn't make much sense to Tony.

Checking his phone, he saw Kristen had messaged him.

'Where are you and Penelope?' it read.

Tony tapped back a simple response, 'Leaving SLO now to get her. She's at my workshop. Bring her to you?'

Tony set the phone on the magnetic charger in his truck and started the engine. He was soon on the road to Los Osos.

KRISTEN DIDN'T BELIEVE what Rodrigo had said of Tony. Every fiber of her soul confirmed the young man couldn't commit such acts. But the detective had lit the logic centers of Kristen's mind, and she continued to doubt herself. A month ago, the very notion of a supernatural intervention being attributed to …well, anything… would have infuriated the psychologist, and she would have discredited it without a moment's hesitation. However, that was before Kristen had experienced a series of events for which she could no longer account.

Still, scientific logic insisted that a ghost couldn't be the answer, and Rodrigo had offered the simplest hypothesis: Tony was the only man they knew of who could have easily committed the crimes. Tony was in the house with her father. Tony had a key to the front door and could have readily been waiting when she and Ryan had come home last night. But Tony wasn't in the bathroom; surely, Kristen would've seen him. Thoughts of being heavily intoxicated haunted her as she attempted to disregard the fact. The hangover still pounded dully through Kristen's exhausted head fifteen hours later.

When the woman arrived at the storage park that housed Tony's workshop, she navigated her sedan to the very back behind the long series of tall silver storage structures. The fluorescent orange garage door of his studio was closed, and the only parked vehicle nearby was the refurbished bus in which he lived. Kristen pulled up in front of the garage door and switched her engine off.

Kristen felt her circulation catch in her legs and stood up from the car to stretch them. The morning's events had exhausted her to the bone, but fear ensured her heart-rate remained elevated. Looking at the storage door, she saw it was padlocked. If Penny were inside his studio, as Tony's message claimed, Kristen couldn't get to her until he arrived.

In a moment of clarity, Kristen looked around her; she was utterly alone. The closest other person was hundreds of feet away towards the front of the storage park. But none of them could see or likely hear Kristen if she needed help. The woman's mind raced, and she searched for a weapon, anything that might offer leverage in a fight. With as many rape victims as the psychologist had counseled, it infuriated Kristen she had nothing in her purse with which to protect herself.

Kristen heard a vehicle approach and panic set in, freezing her limbs. All she could seem to do was watch the navy blue pickup approach.

Tony pulled his aging truck alongside Kristen in front

of the garage door to his studio. He looked stoic as he parked the vehicle, the breeze from his open driver's window carrying wisps of his loose hair into his eyes. Tony only glanced at Kristen for a moment before opening the door to stand up from his truck. Closing the door gently, he approached her and reached to place his arms around her.

It was a caring gesture, and Kristen could feel his warmth and strength, but she couldn't relax into his embrace.

"I'm so sorry," Tony whispered with a somber timbre.

For a moment, she allowed his long embrace to continue, feeling the ice in her limbs begin to recede.

"Did you do it?" Kristen asked him pointedly.

Tony pulled back slowly to release her. A confused expression animated his handsome face.

"Did you kill them?" she asked again, anger stifling Kristen's last word.

"What do you mean?" he asked her, blinking at the unexpected sound of her question.

"Someone killed them," she answered. "Someone killed my father, and then killed Ryan in precisely the same way."

"I don't understand," Tony pleaded quietly. "You told me your father fell and died because no one was there to help him. You said it was an accident."

"I said that," Kristen began to tremble. "But then Ryan fell by accident and died in the same spot, with the very same wound? Someone had to have struck them down, and you were the only one who could've done it. My father let you into the house, probably the very day he died. You're the only one with a key to the house! Why?! Tell me why you did it!"

"I didn't!" Tony answered with terror in his eyes. "I would never hurt Richard! I wouldn't that to anyone."

Tony began to panic—Kristen could see all the signs. His breathing became strickened and shallow. His body fidgeted and jerked as if he were being physically attacked. The man was afraid.

From inside the studio, Kristen heard Penelope bark wildly. The sound broke Tony's focus, and he seemed at a loss to get ahold of himself. Were there tears forming in his eyes? Kristen couldn't be sure before he turned from her to approach the garage door, reaching in his jeans to find the keys to unlock it.

When Tony had removed the padlock, he dropped it and lifted the rolling door up above his head. At once, Penelope sprinted out, encircling her alpha, jumping into action to understand why they had shouted. Tony dropped to one knee and reached to calm the animal, stroking her head lovingly. Penelope licked at his face, then behind his ears, and then focused on his eyelids.

"Hello, sweetheart. We're okay. It's okay," he told her calmly.

Kristen had known when she'd seen his reaction to her accusation. He couldn't have done it, any of it. She'd already known this, of course, known perfectly well that the man couldn't harm anyone. But the detective had made her hesitate. Kristen's fear had made her doubt herself, and her body still trembled from that fear.

"Go see mommy," Tony said quietly to the Husky, and she instantly sprang to Kristen.

The woman received her pet's exuberance with shaky arms that weakly caught the animal's front paws. Kristen followed Tony's example and lowered to the ground so Penelope could properly attend to her mother. She stayed on the ground for some time, not only to allow the dog to release her joy but also to let Tony compose himself. In time, he approached them both, and Kristen finally looked up at his honest eyes.

"I didn't do anything to them," said Tony firmly, and he stared at Kristen, the pain threatening to take over again.

Kristen stood up and approached the young man. She reached around his waist and laid her head on his chest.

"I'm sorry. I know you didn't," Kristen whispered.

The woman began to weep, slowly at first, then quite desperately as the pain shot through her. The weight of her agony overtook Kristen as it seldom could. Had it been Tony's unexpected emotion that released Kristen's well, like her patients so often did during counseling? Her training had allowed the psychologist to understand their pain better—their suffering often overwhelmed her—but she had grown that skill at a high personal cost. Kristen's overdeveloped empathy muscles seemed to block the doctor from feeling the brunt of her own emotional pain. For all she knew, a severed limb might not induce a tear from the doctor. But as she pulled the young man's chest to her, the horrors of Kristen's life broke through and overcame her, drawing out an uncontrollable wailing.

In time, Kristen felt the rhythm of Tony's breathing slow, and his arms enfolded her again.

CHAPTER SIX

Before leaving to drive back the house, Kristen and Tony spoke candidly about the day's events and her plans for the coming week. She apologized to the young man repeatedly for accusing him of betrayal. It became something of an obsession for Kristen—if Tony thought for a moment she didn't believe him, the woman would never forgive herself. She became fiercely protective of him, if that made any sense. Tony filled a place of darkness in her life, and Kristen couldn't be more grateful for his loyalty.

Ryan's face flashed in her mind constantly throughout the day, desperate as she was to avoid the agony with which his memory wounded her. She was in no fit state to return to work, and after she properly strapped Penelope into the back-seat dog harness, Kristen dialed her job during the ride back to the house. She requested a leave of absence from her employer for not less than a month. Kristen described candidly how a close friend of hers had died in her house in the night, and that she couldn't suitably resume her duties now. Kristen's request would require time for Scripp's Memorial Hospital to determine, but they would contact her within forty-eight hours with their decision.

Arriving at the house, the scene from earlier that morning had disappeared. The emergency and sheriff's vehicles were gone as if nothing had happened. Kristen hadn't wanted to enter the home alone, even with the dog, and she was grateful to have Tony by her side as they stepped in.

At the foot of the stairs, Kristen found an official notice declaring the second level was off-limits, per law enforcement orders. 'Do Not Cross' tape blocked the path, its yellow and black pattern far more imposing than plastic tape ought to be.

"Damn it!" yelled Kristen, agitation threatening to consume her.

She had wanted to move into another bedroom upstairs, but now she couldn't even access them.

"I thought the detective just asked you to stay out of the big room," commented Tony.

"She did," answered Kristen, "...but evidently, we're to stay off the whole floor."

"I can get my materials out of the guest room for you. The half-bathroom is a month from being done, but I can probably install the toilet in a couple of days."

Kristen exhaled slowly, her breath labored through her pursed lips.

"And I can't even check into a hotel around here with the dog," she said.

"My gym membership allows me to bring a guest with me," offered Tony. "You can shower there."

Kristen shot him an unsatisfied stare.

"The porta-potty outside is super clean. They just replaced it yesterday, so no one's been in there but me."

The sincere expression on his face sent Kristen into a

volley of hysterical laughter. It was the first genuine release from the day's nightmare, and Kristen didn't attempt to stifle it.

Tony, didn't say anything, but eventually smiled to see the pain finally leave her eyes.

"Yeah, I guess that's where we're at," said Kristen when the fits had released her. "Well, I have nothing but the clothes on my back, so I'd better go make some magic happen.

Two hours later, Kristen arrived home with half-a-dozen shopping bags in her car. She'd found the local Target store and made her way through the establishment, which thankfully had everything she needed. In the travel section, Kristen found every kind of small toiletry, as well as a towel, pillow, and a set of bedsheets to go with the basic clothes on which she settled. As the house was devoid of furniture outside of the shut master bedroom, Kristen also invested in a blow-up mattress, which required only a power socket to bring to life. Beyond finding the motor's 'On' button, Kristen didn't trust herself to figure out much more about the camping device. From the department store's grocery section, Kristen pulled an unwise but necessary selection of comfort foods: Oreo Cookies, Nutella, Lay's Potato Chips, a pack of Coca-Cola, and bottles of water. Kristen felt prepared to survive an apocalypse, at least for a day or two.

Kristen made her way directly to the garage where the washer and dryer waited for her. She chose to start with her new clothes and the towel, color mismatching be damned. If she never made it to the sheets before nightfall, at least she could go with Tony to have a shower at his gym.

When she returned to the car, Kristen found the remaining bags had made their way into the house, courtesy of Tony's generous attention. When she arrived at the downstairs guest room, he was already unraveling the blow-up bed to set it up.

"This is a good one," Tony said when he noticed her. "I'm surprised you didn't have to go to a sporting goods store to find it."

Tony had already cleared the drop-cloths from the space and vacuumed the floor for Kristen. He'd even unmasked the craftsman wall lamps to give her light in the room.

"Target is not wanting for much," she acknowledged. "Thank you for doing all of this, Tony."

"It's no problem," he smiled before flipping the switch that engaged the bed's internal motor.

They both stared at the mattress as it quietly began to inflate, somewhat hypnotized by the modern marvel. Within three minutes, they were presented with a fully-realized, queen-sized bed that was ready to welcome a weary traveler.

"Crazy," Tony laughed. "When I was a kid, we'd have to pump by hand for an hour just to get a bed half this size filled with air."

He laid down on the bed, only to rise out of it immediately.

"Sorry, I just wanted to see how strong it was," Tony said. His reddening face acknowledged what his actions implied louder than any words.

"That's fine," responded Kristen, silently amused by his swiftness.

"Did you want me to take you to the gym for a shower," Tony asked, "before the late afternoon crowd shows up?"

"I need two hours for the clothes to wash and dry first," she answered.

"Sure, that's cool," he nodded.

"Do you want to take Penelope for a walk in the meantime?" she asked. "It doesn't have to be anything special."

"Yeah," Tony smiled. "I'll go change into my gym clothes and see what she's up for."

"I truly appreciate it," Kristen offered warmly and exhaled with defeat. "I don't know what I would've done today without you here."

"You got it," answered Tony, and he left her alone in the room.

Kristen sat down on the bed in time, startled by its flexibility. It would be a strange sensation, the way it moved on account of weighing so very little. She laid down, her head falling on the pillow, still wrapped in plastic, and heard the crinkling in her ears.

Damn it, she thought, *I don't have a blanket*. It seemed she was going to be relying on that Husky for some severe cuddling when the night air rolled in. Luckily, Penelope was a furnace with a double coat.

While Kristen looked up at the ceiling, counting through her internal checklist, she again allowed herself to think of Ryan, of what she'd seen. Burned into her mind was the horrifying image of his lifeless body lying upon the bathroom floor, as was the noxious smell. But he stayed with her only for a few minutes before the exhaustion of this miserable day pressed her eyelids closed.

CHAPTER SEVEN

He couldn't remember exactly when it happened, but Valon realized there were people in his house. The silence of his world came to a startling end, and for the first time in years, he recalled that he was alive.

Workers arrived frequently and hammered down the missing floorboards his father had never finished. On the walls, they installed panels of intricately constructed wainscoting, which they stained with dark oil and polished to a marvelous shine. On the ceiling, they enhanced the ornamental beams to delineate downstairs rooms, always darkening the wood to that of gleaming molasses. They inlaid ornate tin and copper tiles, sculpted lovingly to glimmer in the light.

The work reminded Valon of his grandfather's house in northern California. This was the style his father had tried to recreate before dying, to mirror the home in which Dad had grown up. But Valon didn't want to think of that. Recalling such memories was still too painful a journey into his wounded mind. Aligning the fragments into a cohesive thought was exhausting. All the young man wanted to do now was watch the changes being made to his father's house.

Valon didn't speak to them, the men who walked through his home each day. Instead, he quietly wandered through the house, observing what they did, absorbed in each brushstroke of paint or screw turned.

It was purely an accident when Valon moved a small glass figurine, reaching only to feel its texture. He couldn't remember being able to move things with his touch, but he had seen his hand stir the small object on the shelf where it stood. Valon was so excited by the moving porcelain sculpture of a bashful Japanese geisha that he waved at it in manic determination. However, he couldn't make it move again.

What had he done the first time? Valon tried in vain to recreate the unintended flick of his wrist that had shaken the smiling woman. And then, he saw the figurine move again. The young man hadn't touched it with his hand but had concentrated his thoughts, imagining it move right before it did.

Again, Valon focused, imagining the little painted lady sliding forward, and like that, the geisha fell from the shelf and landed on the hardwood floor to shatter into tiny pieces.

It was this very moment when Valon first noticed her.

A woman with red hair walked up beside him and stared down at the floor in visible frustration. She knelt to pick up the small pieces that had once been the bashful white-faced geisha standing gracefully in her crimson kimono. The red-haired woman tried to reassemble the pieces, but she quickly gave up the impossible task with a huff. Instead, she carried the tiny shards to a nearby trashcan into which she chucked them.

A telephone rang, pulling the woman from her

resentful stare, and she walked to the living room to sit down on the armchair beside it. She lifted the green plastic handset from its base, ending the terrible clanging sound it made.

"Good afternoon," said the woman. "Oh, hello, dear. No, I've just finished unpacking, more or less."

Valon looked around the living room to realize the house was no longer filled with workmen or their tools and materials. Instead, the house appeared complete and filled with furniture. Chairs and tables of various types, an old dark green velvet sofa, large oriental rugs, and a large television set was sitting in the corner. On the tables and the walls were picture frames of various makes and sizes. In many, the red-haired woman stood beside a tall man with dark brown skin and a gleaming smile. He was very handsome, this man—well-built and dressed impeccably in each photo. The man was her husband, Valon expected, a belief supported by a large picture of them standing together in a church, the woman's red hair contrasting against the white of her satin gown.

"If you'd called me a minute earlier," she continued, "I might've been a little happier. I just broke my favorite figurine. Yes, that one—little Kumiko. I don't know, she just fell off the shelf and shattered. I must've placed her too close the edge. Yes, I doubt I'll ever find another as lovely."

The woman's sharp alto couldn't hide her disappointment. On the table beside her, he saw a small pile of letters that sat unopened. The name printed on most of the letters was 'Mr. Bobby Hill.' Each envelope had a yellow sticker affixed to the front, indicating it had been forwarded from a previous address. Valon saw the letters had been initially mailed to somewhere in San Jose. On one, the recipient's name was 'Mrs. Pamela Hill.'

"I love it," she said, "it's a cute little town. No, I do love it—I'm not just saying that. Yes, I miss you terribly. No, but I'm serious, this is exactly what I wanted. A small, out-of-the-way place where I can grow flowers and vegetables and learn to cook like a great chef."

Valon observed the woman's face. There was tension around her lovely green eyes, and they rolled as if she wanted to hurl an insult at the caller.

"Why would you say that?" asked Pamela with exasperation. "That doesn't matter to me. I'm not here to look for someone else, Trish. I'm here because he wanted this for us. He worked sixteen hours a day, six days a week, for thirty years so we could be here."

The mask of her aggravation melted away, and tears collected in her eyes. Pamela closed them tightly and drew her hand to her face. Her chin trembled in pain.

"Trish, I've got to go," she said bluntly and summarily dropped the receiver on its cradle.

In seconds, the telephone rang again. Pamela lifted the receiver and slammed it down. She then raised it again and placed the receiver on the table beside the telephone base so the caller couldn't bother her.

Pamela wept in agony over a wound that was far from healed. When her eyes opened again, she stared out of the living room windows at the trees on the street, following them as they swayed in the gusts of ocean breeze coming from half a mile away.

She attempted to wipe at her eyes, but she saw her mascara had run on her fingers. Frustrated, Pamela rose from her chair and walked upstairs.

Valon followed her, soon finding the woman standing in her bathroom, wiping at her eyes with facial tissue. She stared at herself, a look of exhaustion on her weary face. Pamela opened the medicine cabinet door and stared at two small amber plastic bottles. She lifted one that said 'Hydrocodone' and fumbled to remove the white lid from its top. When she'd managed to get it off, Pamela turned the bottle gently to release one of the large white pills onto the palm of her hand.

After a moment's consideration, she turned the bottle over, letting the rest of its contents empty into her palm. Pamela stared at the mound of white oval pills in silence, a glaze of determination falling over her face. She drew deep, uneven breaths while her green eyes focused on the medication.

"She'll think it was her fault," Pamela whispered to herself.

In time, the woman lifted her palm to return the large white pills carefully into the amber bottle, aside from one dose she held back to place in her mouth. Pamela closed the cabinet door and found herself staring back in the mirror.

Sadness animated her face again.

Filling a glass cup with water from the faucet, she took a healthy sip and swallowed it down with the fat pill. Returning the glass to the sink top, Pamela washed and dried her hands and went to lay down in the bedroom.

She didn't bother to close the blinds; the midday light seemed to be of no concern. Pamela turned her head to glance at the photo of her husband, which sat in a silver frame by the bed, then closed her eyes.

Valon watched all of this with wonder, feeling unexpected empathy for the woman.

When Pamela's breathing had settled into a slow rhythm, Valon sensed she was asleep. And then something happened that he didn't quite understand. Valon could see a faint light emanating from her face. More specifically, he saw the light coming from just above

Pamela's eyes. Mesmerized by the sight, Valon sat down on the bed and brought his eyes right to Pamela's, seeking to look as carefully into the bewildering blaze as he could. When he did this, the light from Pamela's head brightened, and in moments, he felt himself falling into it.

Down Valon fell toward a magnificent source of light that consumed all other things. Within his field of vision, he soon saw an image. It was the face of a man covered in perspiration. The man was Bobby. He stood on a concrete driveway beside an emerald lawn and raised his hand to wipe the sweat from his brow. The day was hot, and he was working on his Corvette's engine, the rumbling sound of which Valon could finally distinguish from the rush of white noise coming from every direction to overwhelm his senses.

"I love you," Valon said to Bobby teasingly, and the man turned to notice.

Bobby's eyes lit up when he saw Valon, and he reached inside the car to switch its motor off.

"You love me?" Bobby said, approaching Valon, who stood on the front porch.

Bobby took Valon's hand and pulled it towards the front door.

"What are you doing?" Valon asked with a sly giggle.

"Someone told me you love me," Bobby answered mockingly and closed the front door behind them.

Bobby pulled Valon close to him and leaned to kiss his sweetheart.

"Stop it, no," Valon smiled. "Trish and Luca are coming over in twenty minutes. You'll mess up my makeup."

"You forget I was on the track team in high school? You think I don't know how to win a race?" asked Bobby as he found Valon's lips.

When the two lovers joined, Valon felt a change. It was as if he were spun around, gravity pulling at him from every direction, so that he almost lost his balance. Opening his eyes, Valon saw Pamela's face, her eyelids closed in rapture as he kissed her erotically. His hands held onto Pamela's frame and soon gripped her bottom, savoring the plump flesh through her lime green skirt. Valon felt a magnetic heat surge through him, raising his heartbeat and stiffening his cock. He was attracted to Pamela in a way he'd never been with another woman.

He needed her.

Valon pulled on the shoulder straps of her dress and bra, just firmly enough to expose her right breast without ripping the garments, and cupped it firmly to bring the hardening nipple to his lips. Pamela stopped her protestations and fell backward on the dark green velvet sofa, surrendering to his wet suckling. She closed her eyes as their bodies found that sweet rhythm that stoked the fire between them.

Valon lifted Pamela's skirt higher and higher, his fingers soon finding her sex to massage her. His sweet invasions raised her breathing, and he soon felt her wetness. Dropping to his knees, Valon spread Pamela's legs to expose her and set about on her sex with his mouth, flicking generously at her with his tongue. It was something Valon enjoyed doing more than anything, giving his wife this sublime joy. And the moans catching in her throat drove him mad with desire for her.

When he could stand it no further, he released his cock from his trousers and brought it to her sex. Valon watched in rapt attention as he rubbed the dark black organ against Pamela's fired pink sex. He coated himself in her wetness until he could stand it no longer and drove into her.

Pamela let out a stifled scream as her sex opened to

receive his hard cock, its fat girth stretching the soft steel of her walls, the intense pleasure diving Valon insane. He could think of nothing more than this focused sensation; this need to drive into her and make the blinding pleasure happen.

Again and again, Valon pushed into her, chasing the fire as long as he could, then slowed himself when the heat came too close. For how long he did this, Valon couldn't have said. It seemed there was nothing outside of this act, this astonishing pleasure, that the man could perceive.

When he could control himself no longer, he surrendered to the fire and let it consume him with a riot of ecstasy that overtook every limb in his body.

As he kissed her, Valon soon felt the waves of pleasure release from his spent body. When he finally opened his eyes again, Valon realized that they were both lying in her bed, their bodies wrapped into each other, and Pamela was staring at him.

Pamela stopped kissing him to gaze at his face in confusion and wonderment. Her eyes filled quickly with uncontrolled tears that fell over her cheeks.

"You've come back to me," she whispered with fragile elation.

"Someone told me you love me," Bobby whispered to her with his usual, gentle smirk.

At once, her frame began to tremble, and Pamela wept uncontrollably as she held to her husband's body, burying her face into his neck.

"Thank God," she sobbed. "Thank you, God."

CHAPTER EIGHT

Kristen's mind did its best to hold onto the dream, willing herself to delve deeper and bring back the lovers' embrace. However, the light streaming through the uncovered window proved too strong to resist, and it pulled her back to consciousness. When Kristen opened her eyes, she found the man was lying beside her. He was not Bobby Hill, but the man Kristen had repeatedly seen in her dreams, and during those seconds just past the threshold of waking.

His name was Valon.

He appeared to her as solidly as any other object in the house. His steel-blue eyes watched Kristen lovingly, and his fingers smoothed her red curls back from her eyes. For the first time, Kristen was not afraid of him, and she gazed at his striking face without the slightest glimmer of concern. Kristen felt safe with him by her side. She was perhaps never more at ease or content in her life.

A noise came from outside the guest room, the tapping footsteps of a dog moving through the house. Penelope and Tony had returned from their walk.

Valon's face moved as if he were about to speak, but

no words came from him. When Penelope rounded the corner and passed through the opened door, Valon disappeared right before Kristen's eyes. She felt the air mattress shift as the weight of him was no longer present.

The Husky entered the room at nearly a manic pace, agitated by something she was wildly intent on discovering. Could Penelope sense him? Sniffing around the floor until she was satisfied, the dog shortly hopped up on top of the air mattress, causing it to wobble a bit before licking Kristen's face devotedly. Penelope then circled in place three times before landing beside her mother to assume her nap-time position.

Kristen watched Penelope without moving, still comforted by the lingering caress of Valon's hand, its warmth not yet gone. In time, the animal closed her eyes, and Kristen took the cue to rise gently from the bed. While the woman's movement alerted the dog's lazy eyes, Penelope didn't move any other muscle in response and soon shut them again. Kristen reached for her tablet and crept from the guest room to check on the laundry.

She thanked Tony again as she passed him. He was already back at work, focused on the kitchen ceiling.

"Probably another hour," she updated him when she headed outside to make her way to the garage.

"Very good," he answered with a vague nod, wholly absorbed with his crafting.

In the garage, Kristen transferred the wet items to the dryer and filled the washer with her new sheets. When both machines were rumbling away, she fired up her iPad. On the screen, Kristen opened her iCloud file of published research on various topics related to the paranormal. Dissatisfied by her initial review, the woman soon went back to the scientific search engines to find more data.

There must be types of ghosts, she reasoned, types of hauntings that resembled her experiences.

This can't be real, Kristen thought angrily as her mind closed to reject the very word 'ghosts.' The psychologist's knee-jerk reaction forced her eyes from the screen. But after a moment of sulking, she pushed past the wall of doubt and forced herself to look at the search results.

Kristen realized that seeking another appointment with her therapist was futile; she must figure this out on her own. How could this be a delusion? She had never experienced such a hallucination before her father passed away. But why this delusion? Why a ghost who fornicates with women while they sleep? Kristen didn't want to allow the word 'rape' to enter her internal monologue, but wasn't that what this was? Why would she have delusions about getting ghost-raped? The very idea infuriated Kristen. Why not a delusion about puppies or kittens or the perfect slice of pizza with extra cheese and no calories to speak of?

As difficult as it was for her to entertain the concept of an afterlife, Kristen realized if she were to get her feet dirty with pseudoscience, she might as well dive headlong into every recorded experience she could find. Over the next hour, she amassed white papers on every type of ghost, apparition, or demon she could from the academic universe.

Kristen made a note of the contact information for several published researchers. She would write a letter to each of them tomorrow. With any luck, the Psy. D. initials after her name would persuade them to take her assistance request seriously.

Swiping to close her applications, Kristen noticed her podcast was still open to the conspiracy theory comedy show she'd listened to that first night with Penelope by her side. The *Wait, Whaaat?* show was hosted by two mothers who loved to talk about their favorite paranormal stories while highly caffeinated.

Kristen realized their weekly podcast was recorded purely for entertainment purposes, but she guessed they might still be a useful source. They'd already devoted several episodes to the subject of ghosts and hauntings. Perhaps they could reference her toward other avenues of research to investigate. She found her way through Google to the show's website, finding their email address.

The loud dryer buzzer announced its cycle had finished, startling Kristen. She would begin her many emails this evening when she returned from the gym. Kristen turned off her tablet and collected her new clothes. She made her way back to the house and let Tony know she was ready for her complimentary shower at his gym.

CHAPTER NINE

The sparkling clean Kim's Plumbing van thrilled Tony into a nervous dance when it pulled up the driveway to park. Though Andrew Kim wasn't the first tradesman to arrive on the worksite, nor the first to work in the house since Tony had taken over the remodel design, the man was the first contractor Tony had hand-picked for the job. The former design firm had engaged the rest of them, and after Tony's management of those contractors had resulted in conflicts, he was eager to build a team of his own. Kristen had given Tony full control of both the design and execution of the refurbishment, an even more excellent opportunity than he'd initially proposed to Richard Cole. For Kristen, Tony had traded an indefinite work timetable for a six-month schedule that came with a budget large enough to use other professionals to realize his vision. This meant Tony would get both his portfolio and the site-management experience he needed in less than half a year. Though Kristen had only agreed to a limited remodel, Tony intended to achieve his original plans for a complete resurrection of the dilapidated craftsman-styled house.

While he would direct and oversee Kim's work on their plumbing needs, Tony would also work every day to apply his woodwork artistry toward the home's aesthetic.

Tony didn't wait for the man to make his way to the front door and proceeded outside to introduce himself.

"Good morning!" he beamed a greeting toward the stocky middle-aged plumber.

"Are you Tony?" Kim asked.

"Yes, welcome," he acknowledged. "I'm so glad you could start with such short notice."

"Well, like I said," answered Kim, "I'm not sure how soon I'll be able to begin the job. But I'm happy to review the house to determine what's needed."

"Excellent!" said Tony with an embarrassingly bright tone. "You might not remember me, but I worked on a job you finished in Atascadero last year. We were only in the house for one afternoon together, but once you were gone, I overheard the site manager discussing with the client how thrilled they were with your work."

"Bartolo Bauer?" Kim asked.

"Yes, that's right," said Tony enthusiastically.

"That's very kind of you to say. He never bothered to mention that to me."

"He said you saved their ass when you found issues he and the designer had overlooked."

"I sure did," declared Kim. "You'd think I would've heard about another job from the guy by now."

"I'm sure one's coming, but I'm glad I got ahold of you first," Tony laughed. "Like I mentioned, another contractor started this job, but it didn't work out. I don't have any reason to believe the man didn't know what he was doing, but he had a challenge meeting the homeowner's needs. And that long story ended when she fired the designer who hired him. Between you and me, I don't think you'll have any challenge with this job, and we're ready for you to start yesterday."

Tony understood his words amounted to a blank check to any contractor, but Tony also recognized that nothing was more crucial to the success of this restoration than its plumbing. Even if the man ripped apart his budget, Tony couldn't afford for the work to fall apart two years from now—not if he was to use this house as the centerpiece of his résumé.

"All right, then. Let's go see what you've got," Kim answered, offering up his first smile in return.

Tony guided the plumber inside the house, opening the front door for the man with a deferential nod. The tour began in the kitchen, where Tony reviewed the preliminary work already done.

From the backyard, Penelope began to bark when she sensed the new arrival in her house, and Tony addressed her swiftly through the glass door, signaling for the Husky to sit down. The animal's hind legs promptly met the wooden planks of the porch, and she silenced herself.

Tony then showed Kim his cabinetry blueprints, ready to be installed once the plumbing was completed, and the fixtures selected for the primary and island sinks.

"This all looks like it will finish up great, and your previous plumber's work looks solid from what I can see," Kim offered.

The acknowledgment lifted a massive amount of anxiety from Tony's shoulders.

The tour then moved on to the downstairs bathroom, where Kim reviewed the existing piping. The man seemed confident he would need to replace the main flow entry under the house. To each comment, Tony nodded and asked Kim to explain why he had made that suggestion. The plumber, clearly accustomed to accounting for his opinions, was happy to enlighten Tony as to his reasoning. As Kim spoke, Tony found himself more and more confident that he had made the right decision. He prayed that the plumber's final bid would make everyone happy.

When Kim took over the tour and moved the men back through the living room to the staircase, Tony snapped out of his daydreaming and spoke up.

"Andrew, I'm afraid we must cut it short here for now. The upstairs bathroom isn't available to us at the moment."

Perplexed, Kim looked to the staircase, noticing the black and yellow 'Do Not Cross' police tape blocking his path.

"What's this?" the man asked with a visible alarm.

"A guest of the owner had a terrible accident yesterday, and I'm afraid he passed away," answered Tony. "The police were here and needed to investigate because of how the poor guy bought it. They've asked us to stay off the top floor while they finish up their investigation. I'm not sure exactly how long it will take, but I don't expect it will impede your work. They're bound to finish well before you start. There's a hall bathroom upstairs that's identical to the one you just reviewed."

Kim appeared speechless while Tony elaborated, but hit to the jugular when the young man finished.

"What sort of accident?" Kim asked.

"I don't really know, to be honest," claimed Tony, and he smiled nervously in response to the man's suspicious stare. "But I'm told their investigation is standard procedure when someone dies from anything but old age in a nursing home."

Kim seemed to take the explanation poorly, looking down at his clipboard and haphazardly notating something Tony guessed read, 'Murder House: +25%.'

"There's not much here for me," acknowledged Kim in a reversal of his earlier tone. "I'll look at my schedule and send over an estimate if I can find an opening."

Tony's heart quietly sank.

"I really would appreciate it," the young man offered.

Kim turned to leave, but then his manners got the better of him, and he extended his hand out to Tony.

"Good luck," the man said curtly.

"Thank you for coming out," said Tony with as grateful a delivery as he could muster, sure he'd just been stood up.

From the living room windows, he watched Kim make his way back to his van and depart.

"Fuck me," Tony whispered to himself in a tone of pure defeated.

From the backyard, Penny began to bark wildly, drawing Tony's attention with alarm. Before he could attend to the distraction, Tony heard Kristen emerge from the downstairs guestroom and walk toward the kitchen. When the poor woman came into view, Tony saw she looked flustered and sweaty, her flaming red hair a mess, as if she'd woken up after running a marathon.

When Kristen approached the glass kitchen door to attend to Penny, she turned the door handle to be firmly pushed backward. The Husky barreled past her into the house like an avalanche. Penelope's paws slipped and struggled to gain traction as she turned through the small hallways that brought her to the guestroom door. The dog only remained in the room for a moment before continuing her mad advance around the bend towards the downstairs coat closet.

The Husky barked wildly at the door, releasing a snarl as if she were preparing to rip an intruder's throat out.

She swiped at the door angrily, attempting to get inside at whatever had drawn her there.

Kristen didn't make a sound as this happened but stood with a look of frozen concern.

Tony approached Penny and called her name sharply, breaking the Husky's focus long enough to acknowledge her alpha's address.

"Sit down," he told her firmly, and the animal's hind legs arrived on the floor without hesitation. "All the way," he added, and Penelope extended her front paws to bring her belly down level with visible impatience at the order. "Good girl."

Tony reached for her collar and walked the dog out of the house, returning her to the extended leash, which Kristen must have failed to attach correctly this morning.

"Good girl?" Kristen said to Tony as he returned to the coat closet.

"You see all this?" he pointed to the scratches on the door.

Penelope had repeatedly attempted to get inside the closet over the past two weeks.

"I wasn't paying attention," he admitted, shaking his head.

Tony opened the closet and peered into the dark space. When the lamp didn't respond after he flicked the switch, the young man looked up to realize he hadn't remembered to replaced the bulb since that first day when it exploded. He would see to it today, as they had a problem that required immediate attention.

"We've got rats," he said to Kristen and exhaled with even more defeat than when Kim had walked out on him. "I'd bet my life on it."

CHAPTER TEN

Kristen arrived at the Paso Robles Target department-store parking lot with a shopping list of various rodent extermination and prevention items composed by Tony. Having used a flashlight to investigate the living room coat closet better, he declared there were no droppings to be found. But that wasn't exactly great news.

Tony trusted Penelope's instincts and firmly believed the house had unwelcome pests. The lack of visual evidence made it likelier that the rats were only inside the walls. Attempting to battle against an embedded infestation could mean thousands of dollars in repairs. The first thing Tony did was to contact the local Terminix branch to schedule an appraisal appointment.

But Kristen had rather spectacular doubts as to the cause of Penelope's aggression. Kristen believed her Husky could sense Valon and knew where the ghost was in the house.

After Kristen let the animal out in the morning, she returned to bed with the explicit goal of allowing Valon to return to her. The woman suspected the ghost could only come to her when she was asleep and dreaming. Though Kristen could still see Valon for moments after awakening, he'd never arrived without first communicating through her dreams. When she returned to bed, Kristen again experienced the dream of Pamela and Bobby Hill. The identical sequence played, allowing Kristen to realize sooner she was dreaming as it played out. And, once again, Kristen had awoken with Valon lying beside her on the air mattress.

When Valon again attempted to speak to her, the words wouldn't come. His lungs seemed locked, unable to pass breath through his throat to create sound. At that moment, Penelope's vicious barking erupted from the backyard, and Valon disappeared.

The experiences left Kristen determined to communicate with the ghost. While the dreams were vivid and deeply impactful, Kristen knew she couldn't remember everything in them. Some fragments resisted recall, and the conscious assemblage of what she could remember often felt incoherent. Kristen still couldn't quite remember the dream of when Valon had been alive in the house. He had felt eager to hold something stolen, some piece of jewelry. As much as Kristen tried, she couldn't recall why it was so important to him or what had happened to it.

Kristen's mind thought of nothing else as she parked her car, staring aimlessly forward. Her mind hit wall after mental wall in its attempt to recall the details. Kristen couldn't have said how long she sat there pondering about Valon before a dark image distracted her.

She looked to the rear-view mirror to find a black lifted Ford F20 truck with big, knobby tires park in the space directly behind her across the lane. A shorter woman dropped from the relatively lofty height of the driver's seat. Kristen couldn't hold back a smile as the four-foot-tall woman stood next to the nine-foot-tall vehicle.

Back to the present task at hand, Kristen rose from her sedan and made her way into the driveway lane to begin her walk toward the department store's front doors. A last glance toward the truck resulted in Kristen spotting a bumper sticker on its rear fender. The solitary tag was the logo for the *Wait, Whaaat?* podcast. After examining the sticker for a good while, Kristen noticed the short woman was staring at her.

"I love that show," Kristen smiled with embarrassment.

"Oh, really?" the little Asian woman's eyes lit up. "Thank you! That's my show."

Kristen didn't quite comprehend the woman's statement until she recognized the lady's face from the cover-art of the comedy program. Hers was one of the two faces staring out in mock terror behind the show titles.

"Are you serious?" Kristen asked her.

"Yeah, I'm Elaine," the middle-aged woman pointed quickly to her sternum with a bright grin.

Kristen's mouth dropped for a moment, and she approached.

"Can I buy you a coffee?" Kristen asked. "I need to talk to you about something."

Despite how public recognition had seemed to delight Elaine, the question dimmed the glimmer in her eyes.

CHAPTER ELEVEN

"So, what's your story?" Elaine asked when Kristen reached for the short latte atop the café table between them.

To Kristen's joy, they found a Starbucks coffee shop inside Target's front lobby. It was a lucky bit of converged commercialism, providing a highly visible public setting to quell Elaine's apparent concerns. She likely considered it a safe space for nut jobs to approach her.

"I think my house is haunted," answered Kristen pointedly.

"Oh," Elaine's eyes widened. "What have you seen?"

"Before I tell you, let me first say I'm a clinical psychologist," Kristen admitted. "I'm a doctor who regularly works with patients suffering from various types of mental disorders, many of which produce hallucinations and delusions they entrust me to help them overcome and survive. I'm telling you this upfront so you understand when I say that I'm a hard, verified skeptic about anything to do with the supernatural. Until a few weeks ago, you and I would've never had this conversation."

"Okay, that's cool," Elaine shrugged. "I realize we run

a paranormal talk show, but I'm also reasonably skeptical about all the stuff we discuss. It's often that very skepticism that fuels the comedy on the show. But I still force myself to remain open to the stories and ideas we present."

"I guess I need you to teach me how you do that," Kristen conceded. "My father raised me within the restrictions of a strictly scientific viewpoint, one that demands a concentrated level of irrefutable evidence just to admit that gravity is the reason leaves fall to the ground. There's never been room in my life for ghosts, spirits, or demons. Certainly, none of the things I'm about to share with you."

"I love that," Elaine smiled. "If something's happened that can make you, of all people, question what you know, I'm extremely interested in what you have to say."

Elaine reached for her small blue suede handbag and pulled out her cell phone.

"Do you mind if I record this?" she asked. "I won't play it on the air, or anything. I just don't want to forget anything you tell me."

"Sure, I do the same thing at my job," agreed Kristen. "Let's just call me Krissy—that's what my dad called me. I won't tell you my real name. I'm not willing to let my guard down to that extent."

"Fair enough," offered Elaine, and she searched through her cell phone screens for the voice recording app. "Okay, I think I've got this bad boy going, so I'll lay it here on the table between us."

She positioned the cell phone on the flat surface between their beverages and looked up without a word, ready to hear Kristen's story.

"There's a ghost named Valon who speaks to me through my dreams. He comes to me each time I fall asleep in my house. If my dog is in the room with me, I wake up before the climax of the dream. But if I'm alone, the dreams resolve with sexual intercourse."

"Holy shit!" Elaine's eyebrows raised. "When did this start happening?"

"My father passed away last month, so I've been up in Cambria preparing to sell his house—organizing a renovation. Since the week I arrived, I've had erotic dreams almost every time I sleep, usually about a familiar lover. But near the end of each dream, I realize I'm dreaming. That's when the boyfriend becomes a stranger I've never met before."

"That's the ghost? You called him Valon?" Elaine verified.

"Exactly," Kristen confirmed. "And when I wake up, Valon is lying beside me, looking as real to my eyes as you do at this very moment. And then, moments later, he vanishes right before my eyes."

"Why do you think he vanishes right then?" the woman asked.

"I don't know the answer to that," Kristen admitted. "During the last two days, my dog sensed the ghost and started barking or barreling through the bedroom to protect me from him."

"Wait, back to the intercourse," Elaine blinked. "Do you only have sex with him in the dreams?"

"Mostly, but not always," verified Kristen. "Sometimes, when I wake up, we are still very much having intercourse."

"So, you're awake when he's doing it to you?" she asked.

"I've been awake during intercourse a few times now. Once, I was awake the whole time we made love," said Kristen.

"You're *fucking* with me!" Elaine whispered in shock,

and she picked up her coffee cup, though it had trouble making the journey to her lips.

"He was inside of me, grinding away—then he finished and disappeared," said Kristen. "Valon didn't manually get off me like any other man. I felt the weight of his body cease to press down upon me. He didn't manually pull out—I felt the girth of his penis stop being inside of me when his body disappeared. And I wasn't asleep when this happened, not at all. I remember everything about it, from the sounds to the smells."

"If you thought he was a stranger, how do you know his name is Valon?" Elaine eyed her suspiciously.

"I first read it on some real estate paperwork that listed his name as Valon William. It reported him as being killed in the house back in the 1980s. That kind of incident is something home sellers have to report to property buyers in this county. Later, I had a dream from his point of view, where I experienced how he died and why he's trapped in the house."

"How did he die?" asked Elaine, taking her first genuine sip of the hot latte.

"That's where it gets hazy for me," Kristen sighed. "Fragments of the dream are still in my mind, but I don't clearly see the whole now. What I remember was that he stole something from his job, something valuable. And when he tried to hide it in the house..."

Kristen's eyes looked vacantly to the empty table on her right. She was on the cusp of it, but the event wouldn't come to life in her mind anymore.

"I can't truly remember that part. But I remember how after Valon died and tried to step out of the house, he opened the front door and found nothing—just inky darkness beyond the door frame. The world he could see through the windowpanes didn't exist when he tried to walk out the front door. He's trapped there."

"Sick," Elaine eyed her with fascination.

"There's more," Kristen added. "The last couple of times he was with me, Valon tried to tell me something, but the words got caught in his throat."

"Has he ever spoken to you?" asked Elaine.

"Yes," said Kristen. "I definitely remember him telling me he loved me, that he wants me to stay with him. But the last two times, he seemed bent on saying something else, something important to him, but he couldn't seem to make a sound."

"Wait, so how many times have you been with him?" Elaine asked, sitting back in her chair as if she finally understood that these weren't infrequent experiences.

Kristen stared down at the table, searching through the days of events to arrive at a number.

"I remember at least ten different dreams where Valon made an appearance, and I've seen him five times with my eyes while awake," declared Kristen.

"For fuck's sake!" Elaine eyed Kristen in amazement.

"But you got me off track. The last thing I wanted to tell you was that a couple nights ago, I had my real-life boyfriend, Ryan, over to spend the night. We had been drinking, and before we moved to my bedroom to have sex, Ryan went to use the bathroom. While I was waiting for him, I fell asleep. To be honest, I must've passed out from being so drunk. We had come home from drinking just barely before eight-o'clock and made our way to the bedroom.

"Next thing I knew, I woke to feel Ryan lay down on the bed behind me and touch my body. When I opened my eyes, the digital clock on my bedside read it was just after three in the morning. We made love for half an hour in the dark. Even if I had turned over to look at him, I couldn't really have seen Ryan's face.

"When we finished, Ryan got up from the bed. I turned on the bedside lamp and quickly realized he wasn't in the room. Instead, I saw the light from under the bathroom door and thought I'd simply not heard him go in there. I got up from the bed and waited patiently for Ryan to finish, but I eventually became impatient and knocked on the bathroom door to ask if I could come in to use it. He didn't answer.

"I opened the door and found Ryan lying on the tile floor. He was dead," Kristen said with a numb expression.

"What?!" cried Elaine over the department store noise. "How did he die?"

"The police told me Ryan had died from a concussive head wound," said Kristen, lowering her voice to signal her discomfort at Elaine's volume. "They suspect he fell and hit his head on the bathtub."

"Shit, I'm so sorry," said Elaine, now speaking in almost a whisper. "But wait, how did you not notice that? You didn't hear him fall that hard?"

"I heard him fall at eight o'clock the previous night, not ten minutes before I fell asleep. We were drunk, and he was wobbly from the booze, and I just laughed at the noise of him falling in the bathroom because …I thought it was funny. We were laughing at everything when we came home."

Kristen stopped, overcome to hear herself speak of Ryan's death. It wasn't real to her. It remained locked away in her mind like a dream—a nightmare she couldn't bring herself to analyze. The pain of his loss might kill her, Kristen felt sure of it now, and she fought with every ounce of strength to keep from falling apart.

"The coroner confirmed that Ryan had been dead for several hours when I called the paramedics."

Elaine shook her head in confusion for a moment before the words made sense to her, then stared at Kristen, her eyes registering.

"So, your boyfriend died, and then his spirit came to have sex with you?" Elaine asked.

"No," Kristen answered weakly, "it was Valon who made love to me."

"You're sure?" asked Elaine.

"I wasn't sure when the event was happening, but I am now," acknowledged Kristen. "It was Valon who made love to me in the dark early morning hours."

Elaine didn't respond, her face unresponsive as if frozen by Kristen's story.

"One last thing," she added. "When my father died last month, the police found him dead on the same bathroom floor."

"What?" asked Elaine, the word coming from her mouth as a quiet puff of air.

"The police found him with a head wound that they attributed to his death. They reported Dad must've fallen by accident and hit his head on the bathtub."

Elaine shook her head in horror at Kristen's words.

"And so, the two incidents are being criminally investigated," added Kristen.

"You think it was Valon's doing?" asked Elaine, the question more of a declaration.

Kristen felt tears forming again.

Hearing the words spoken aloud had convinced her more than ever of what the stunned woman had just asked.

"You've got to get out of the house," said Elaine with a raised, assertive tone.

"Why?" asked Kristen, silently laughing as she brought a paper napkin to her eyes to prevent the tears from dropping. "I'm not the one who seems to be in danger."

"Still," demanded Elaine. "You shouldn't take the chance. What if you do something the ghost doesn't like, so he turns on you?"

"I have a feeling that would be the last thing he would do. He's madly in love with me, and when I'm in his arms, I don't feel a care in the world."

Elaine leaned forward and spoke directly at Kristen in slow, broken words.

"Um, this—is—fucked—up," she responded before sitting back again to look at their surroundings.

"What I want now," continued Kristen, "is to communicate with him while I'm awake. I lose myself in him when I'm asleep, and even after I wake, I can't trust my faculties. I heard you talk about using Ouija boards on one of your episodes."

"Oh, *fuck* no!" scowled Elaine. "That's definitely what you don't want to do. Were you even listening? Because I say the same thing every time that word comes out of Paula's lips—stay away from Ouija boards."

Kristen looked in the distance past the line of checkout stands where the department store's shoppers were waiting for service. She scanned the large red and white signs suspended throughout the mammoth building in search of one that read 'Toys & Games.'

"They sell them here, don't they?" asked Kristen.

CHAPTER TWELVE

Kristen arrived home with Tony's requested rodent-prevention supplies, which he gladly paused his plasterwork to take off her hands. She left the Hasbro Ouija Board in the trunk of her sedan, unprepared for Tony to learn about it just yet.

Elaine had scoffed at the invitation to join Kristen for a night of communicating with the dead. The two women had exchanged phone numbers, but Kristen didn't expect to hear from her again. Still, being able to say everything aloud to someone who wasn't a doctor, who would listen purely to disseminate each sentence or expression in search of Kristen's mental illness, had proved to be a massive relief. Keenly motivated to attack this challenge head-on, the woman didn't give her purchase a second thought. Elaine's fear of the Ouija board was all the license Kristen needed to attempt something she would otherwise consider mindlessly foolish.

Kristen received a text message from an unknown number late in the afternoon. The sender identified herself as Paula McCambridge, a friend of Elaine Chaney's, and the co-host of the *Wait, Whaaat? Podcast.*

Paula asked if she might accept Elaine's invitation and join Kristen during her attempt to contact Valon. Without hesitation, Kristen responded with an enthusiastic acceptance and sent back her address.

She asked Tony if he would quit early to accompany her to his gym for another shower. Despite Kristen's initial concerns, she had appreciated the women's locker room at Tony's temple of muscles and sweat, which was spotless and well-appointed. The sensation of being clean again was one Kristen appreciated, especially as she prepared to receive a guest.

When a tall, middle-aged Caucasian woman with dark wavy hair rang the doorbell shortly after eight o'clock that evening, Kristen couldn't help but giggle at the contrast of the woman's size to Elaine Chaney's.

"Paula?" Kristen asked warmly, opening her front door.

"Krissy?" the woman asked back with a sharp midwestern accent. She stood on Kristen's porch in a red plaid flannel shirt and black jeans, clutching a large brown leather purse, almost as if she were relying on the bag as a source of safety.

"Come on in," answered Kristen warmly, unconcerned by assuming her father's private nickname for her.

"I'm so glad to meet you," said Paula. "Elaine shared with me the amazing story you told her, and I just had to meet you."

"It surprised me to hear from you," acknowledged Kristen, "particularly after Elaine's reception to my idea."

"Oh, she and I differ on many things, Ouija boards being at the top of the list," said Paula with a chuckle. "I'm completely fascinated by the idea, but I've never had an opportunity like this—not to use the board in a place where we know there's a spirit present."

Paula stopped, her eyes falling on the staircase blocked by the black and yellow 'Do Not Cross' police tape.

"I listened to the recording, but you didn't mention this," said Paula apprehensively.

"Didn't I? Forgive me; I thought I had. Ryan's death is under investigation by the police," Kristen answered pensively. "He died upstairs in the master bathroom, and the police have asked me to remain downstairs until they finish what they're doing."

"My God, I'm so very sorry for your loss," Paula said, lowering her voice.

Kristen mused that the woman might have just recognized for the first time that she wasn't attending a carnival haunted house.

"Thank you," she acknowledged gratefully.

"So, are we not going to use the board in your bedroom?" Paula asked, visibly perplexed by the notion.

"I moved down to the ground floor guest room," Kristen explained, "and he has visited me there twice since. It doesn't seem to matter where in the house we speak to him, as long as we're in the house when we do."

"Really?" the woman's eyes widened with surprise.

"I've set up the board in the living room," said Kristen. "Let me apologize that I don't have a stick of furniture for us to sit on. As you can see, we're going through a remodel. The only room with any furniture is upstairs. But I laid out a bedsheet for us, so we don't get dirty."

Kristen gestured to the large square of navy linen laid out on the brown butcher-paper drop cloth that covered the entire bottom floor. She had set up the board game at the center of the spartan setting.

"I wanted to go down to the market and pick up something for us but wasn't sure what you'd like. I'm ashamed to say I have nothing in the house to offer you, but I can order us some drinks and nibbles if you'd like. Door Dash should deliver it fairly quickly at this hour," Kristen offered.

"Oh, no, please don't go to any trouble," said Paula with a sharp decline. "I've already had dinner, and I don't drink anymore. Besides, I want my wits about me tonight."

"I feel the same way," agreed Kristen. "Well, is there anything you think we should do before we begin? How much do you know about Ouija boards?"

"Honestly, they're Elaine's area of expertise," Paula admitted sheepishly. "She picks up on every story that comes along on the subject. Even if I bring one to a taping session, she takes over the conversation in no time. But I find them fascinating, and this will be my first time using one."

"Mine, too," acknowledged Kristen. "I've seen them used in movies and television shows, but never in person. I grew up an only child. One parent was a scientist, and the other hated board games. But I remember the girl from *The Exorcist* using it to speak with Satan, who pretended to be her bestie at that point in the movie. I'm fairly certain that was right about when I decided never to touch one."

"Oh, my God," chuckled Paula. "That movie scared the crap out of me when I was a girl. But you're okay with it now?"

"This isn't Satan we'll be talking to," said Kristen, shaking her head. "And if it is, well…"

"Do you want to bring your dog inside?" Paula asked, filing in Kristen's silence.

"No, we'll hear her from the backyard if Valon makes an appearance. I'm certain she can sense him," said Kristen.

"Are there more lights you can turn on?" asked Paula, looking around at the small bulbs shining in the wall sconces of the living room.

"I'm afraid not—the ones that are properly working are already on for us," Kristen assured the woman.

"Maybe Door Dash delivers candles with the booze?" Paula laughed loudly. "Sorry, I'm starting to feel nervous."

"Come on," Kristen smiled, "let's sit down on the floor and get right to it. Have you read the instructions for this thing?" asked Kristen, quickly kneeling to assume a Lotus position.

"No," Paula responded as she made her way down on the ground to join Kristen. She took the manual from beside the board gently as if it were some important relic. "I didn't even think there would be a manual, but I guess that makes sense, huh?"

"I can give you the highlights," said Kristen. "For one, it says we're not pronouncing it properly. It's wee-ja, not wee-gee."

"Oh, I don't like that," said Paula, with a defiant shake of her head. "I don't think I can change at this point. I've been saying wee-gee all my life."

"Me too," said Kristen, "so, to hell with Hasbro. This thing is a wee-gee board, and that's all we'll tolerate."

"Great," nodded Paula.

"Second," Kristen continued, "this thing here is what the ghost moves when we ask it questions. It's called a message indicator, or planchette."

"Ooo, I like that!" Paula's eyes widened. "Planchette. Is that French?"

"I imagine," Kristen shrugged.

"Hold on, I want to look it up," said Paula, and she reached in her handbag for her cell phone. After tapping the word in, she announced, "Mid-nineteenth century;

from French, literally 'small plank,' diminutive of planche. Oh, like on a pirate ship—they execute people by making them walk the plank."

"And on French ships, they walk *ze planche*," said Kristen, affecting her most pretentious French accent.

"Okay, great," Paula said enthusiastically. "The message indicator is a little plank, …and we walk down it to our metaphorical doom."

Kristen let herself give a truthful smile for the first time in days. "Lastly, we're each to place our middle and index fingers lightly on the planchette, then concentrate as we ask questions. We're expected to wait up to five minutes for a response to each question."

"Oh, this will go very slowly if Valon isn't feeling talkative," remarked Paula, scrunching her face humorously.

"I'm gonna give him a solid thirty seconds, don't worry," Kristen assured her with another smile.

Then, they said no more. The two women stared at each other silently for several moments. Paula waited for Kristen to begin. Kristen waited for the nerve to place her fingers on the planchette.

"Oh, wait," said Paula, disturbing the quiet that had set in. "Elaine sent me something she said was very important to read before we begin."

Kristen inhaled at the interruption, realizing that she had slowed her breathing in anticipation.

Paula tapped through her phone to find the messaged document.

"Here we are. These are rules that everyone should know before using a Ouija board," said Paula, squinting at the screen. "Okay, the most important rule is that you must never taunt or goad a spirit, which can be disastrous. Another is to remember that spirits can say anything to you. They can lie just as easily as they can tell the truth, and you should be prepared for a malevolent spirit to try and charm you into believing they're good."

"I'm on to you, Satan," said Kristen, to which Paula giggled nervously.

"Let's see," continued Paula, "never use a Ouija board in your home... Oh, well, I guess we've already fucked that one up."

Kristen snorted despite herself.

"Participants should never remove their fingers from the indicator, and the leader should not ask joke questions," said Paula, looking up at Kristen with concern.

"No promises," Kristen smiled mischievously.

"If the spirit starts to count down through the numbers or alphabet, immediately say 'Goodbye' and release the planchette. That's a demon," said Paula, sticking out her finger as if she were marking a crucial point. "The same goes for the figure eight or infinity symbol, or if the spirit announces himself as 'Zozo,' who's an evil spirit."

One who plays board games, Kristen thought to herself, doubting her decision to use the damned thing more with each word Paula said.

"Never use a Ouija in a cemetery..." Paula's voice faded. "Well, that's a disappointment. What better place is there to talk to the dead? Oh, here's one for you, 'If you are experiencing depression, it may be good to avoid using a Ouija board. That kind of energy draws in malevolent spirits.'"

"That one rings true," said Kristen, not bothering to mention that cases of schizophrenia, where the patient claimed to see or hear spirits, often went hand-in-hand with clinical depression.

Kristen silently placed her fingers on the planchette, giving Paula a moment to finish reading the list of some asshole's mind-control techniques before tapping lightly on the plastic to catch the woman's attention.

"Oh, all right then," said Paula, apprehensively setting her cell phone to sleep before placing it back in her handbag. She exhaled slowly and placed her fingers on the planchette across from Kristen's.

"I am speaking to Valon William," Kristen started with a steady volume. "Are you here? Valon, will you speak with us?"

Kristen waited through the silence, the only response to her question, for ten seconds before she repeated herself. Still, there was no response.

"Valon!" Kristen raised her voice with a disproportionate increase in volume that startled Paula. Kirsten recognized her outburst as impatience rather than concern over whether Valon couldn't hear her.

From the backyard, she heard Penelope release a short volley of barks. However, by now, Kristen could read the color of the Husky's different cries. This sound was an acknowledgment that her mother had raised her voice, something Kristen rarely did.

"She's just barking because she heard me," said Kristen, shaking her head at Paula's concerned look. "I'm sorry I shouted—she just wants to come in and check on me."

"That's not the worst idea I can think of," replied Paula.

"Valon won't come to me if I let Penelope inside," said Kristen, shaking her head again.

"Maybe he's a cat person?" Paula joked.

Kristen didn't answer but gestured to the board with her eyes.

"Wasn't that one of your rules?" the psychologist

asked, staring down at the woman's hands gathered anxiously in her lap.

"Oh, right. Sorry," answered Paula, and she took another deep breath before returning her fingers to the planchette.

Kristen closed her eyes and exhaled. She focused on Valon, seeing his blue-steel colored eyes in her mind. Kristen heard the deep timbre of Valon's voice in her memory, recalling how he'd asked her to stay with him— that he loved her. She remembered the feel of his warm lips on her neck.

"Valon William, I know you're here with me now," said Kristen. "Will you please speak to me through this device?"

Kristen heard the calmly measured sound of her breathing in the room's silence, but she heard nothing else.

CHAPTER THIRTEEN

I t wasn't only that Kristen believed Valon would speak through the Ouija board—she *expected* to hear his voice. But as the evening continued, and Paula attempted her own fruitless invitations to the ghost, the stillness of the Ouija board became infuriating to the psychologist. Kristen knew Valon was in this house, and his silence bothered her deeply.

"Also, the list said that you shouldn't store the planchette with the board," Paula added as she passed over the threshold on her way out.

"You got it," Kristen said as cordially as she was capable of in her agitated state.

However, she failed to prevent the door from shutting a little too aggressively behind the poor woman, and Kristen's embarrassment only served to compound her frustration. When the talk-show host was down the steps and back at her car, Kristen gathered the game and carelessly stuffed it into its glossy cardboard box. She threw the message indicator in with the board, shut the lid, and chucked the whole thing into Tony's worksite garbage pail.

Kristen let Penelope into the house, stoking a riot of joy from the lonely animal. She directed the Husky to the guest room, where Kristen closed the door behind them both and quickly undressed for bed. When they were both snuggled on the air mattress, Kristen lit up her tablet to search for the previous owner of the house, Pamela Hill. While most of the results in Google were useless for-pay information sources, there was one link that seemed to promise a wealth of information on Hill. Kristen then did something she had promised herself she'd never do again.

In the App Store, she searched for Facebook and tapped to download the program. Kristen had tried Facebook only once before. Within a week, the psychologist discovered how eager many patients were to "friend" her in the virtual world. The role of a psychotherapist is not to be a patient's friend but their doctor, guiding them to mental health. However, the desire to connect with someone whose job is to be on a patient's side often proves highly desirable, even if true friendship is not possible. After Kristen had blocked half-a-dozen people, she recognized Facebook was a bad idea for her and pulled the plug on her account.

When the application was up, Kristen tapped to create an account, only to find that Facebook still recognized her from her cellphone number. It reinitialized her old page within seconds as if Kristen had never told it to delete her information years ago.

I won't be on here long enough for it to matter, she thought.

When the page was ready, Kristen typed the name Pamela Hill into the search engine. Within seconds, seventeen women with the same name filled the screen. Tapping on the distance icon, the list resorted itself to place an eighty-six-year-old woman who lived in San Luis Obispo at the very top.

The face in the photo gave Kristen chills. The older woman's once red hair was now pure white, but her face was too similar to be anyone else. She had found Pamela Hill, and half of her postings were geo-tagged from a location called Sunset Villas Retirement Community.

CHAPTER FOURTEEN

The receptionist at Sunset Villas was a young blonde woman named Jessica, according to the large print on her badge, and she displayed visual signs of chemical addiction. She had the slender frame of a twenty-year-old woman, but her skin looked like it had already reached middle-age. Jessica's blue eyes were massively dilated, and the surrounding skin had dehydrated into a sickly pallor that promised to one day make for a lovely zombie.

Methamphetamines, thought Kristen as she watched Jessica fidget nervously through a series of unidentifiable tasks.

"Hey, hello, welcome!" the receptionist said with an explosive start.

"Good morning!" Kristen smiled with matched enthusiasm. "I'm here to visit Pamela Hill."

"Oki-doki," answered the young woman with a slight twitch. "I just need you to sign in here. Are you a relation or friend?"

"I've never met her, but she knew my parents before they died. I've come to deliver the news of their passing,"

Kristen answered as she wrote her personal information into the register.

"Oh, I'm so sorry to hear that," the woman roared with a heavy tone of false sympathy. It seemed to be a phrase Jessica frequently delivered to struggling ears. "She and the other ladies are out in the main hall for recreation just now, so you're welcome to go introduce yourself. Would you like me to take you there and do that for you?"

"No worries, hon, don't bother yourself," Kristen answered with an excited grin. "I know what she looks like. Thank you so much for your help!"

The woman acknowledged Kristen with nothing but pursed lips and a silent nod.

Kristen followed the corridor around the bend to find herself in a large central room where a collection of recliners in mismatched fabrics were scattered throughout. The facility made up in function and cleanliness for what some may have considered a lack of style. Only a few of the inhabitants of this space seemed to be fully awake, those exceptions being a table of women playing cards loudly in the center of the room. A movie playing on a gigantic television screen absorbed the rest.

Kirsten's parents had never come to such a "home," and she secretly felt grateful, even if she would do anything to have her father back.

In the far corner, Kristen found Pamela Hill seated in a green and red scotch recliner. At first, it appeared the chair was pointed at the window so the woman could look out onto the garden, but Kristen soon discovered the real reason for her choice of seats. In Pamela's hands was a small iPad plugged into the electrical outlet on the wall beside her. The woman was reading a novel displayed in a font so large that less than ten words could fit on the screen at any single moment. Pamela's thumb touched the screen with frequent swipes as she pushed the scrolling text of her novel up and up to read through the huge words.

"Pamela?" Kristen asked quietly.

The woman's round face appeared to stutter as her mind came out of the novel to gaze in the young woman's direction. Kristen again felt a chill to see Pamela's eyes staring at her, remembering their intimacy and love from the dream. Her face was fuller, and her hair was now the color of fresh snow, but the luminous blue of her eyes was unmistakable. When she smiled, the sweet roundness of Pamela's cheeks almost put Kristen to tears.

"Yes?" Hill responded, her high voice still ringing like a bell.

"Hello, my name is Kristen," she whispered. "We haven't met before, but you may remember my parents. Richard and Margaret Cole? They purchased your home in Cambria a few years back."

The light in Pamela's eyes darkened for a moment, and she looked down at her tablet to find the button to set it to sleep.

"Are they okay?" she asked, the sweetness of her face all but gone.

"My mother passed away from cancer a couple of years ago," Kristen answered gently. "My father died just last month."

"What took him?" Hill asked pointedly.

Kristen felt unsure of how to respond. She held the woman's gaze for several moments, feeling the pain grow and recede before she could answer.

"Dad had an accident," said Kristen. "He slipped and hit his head."

"In the bathroom?" Hill asked, again with an edge to her query.

"Yes," Kristen answered, feeling paralyzed by the question.

Pamela's eyes at once evoked fear. They shifted erratically, as if to search her mind for some bit of memory, then rose back to Kristen with a glimmer of pain.

"Can you take me out of here?" she whispered. "I must speak to you alone."

"Do you want me to walk you to your room?" Kristen asked.

"No, we can't go there. The staff makes me leave the door open during the day, and I need to tell you something no one should hear," said Hill.

Kristen nodded hesitantly and returned to the reception desk at the front room. Jessica offered little resistance when Kristen expressed her wish to take Pamela out to lunch, making a quick notation in her book. All it took was a promise to have the resident back by four o'clock, and the pair were soon on the road.

Hill was swift to mention where she wanted Kristen to take them. She instructed her emancipator to drive the sedan through downtown San Luis Obispo as if she would know it blind. When Kristen asked what Hill needed to tell her, the woman refused to say, insisting they couldn't be driving for such a discussion. In time, the pair arrived at Novo Restaurant on Higuera Street and snagged a parking spot at the curb only a couple of doors down.

The restaurant appeared to be a small eatery from the street, but Kristen soon found the establishment's real lure was a massive wooden deck behind the main building, supporting dozens of tables under a pair of beautiful old oak trees.

Kristen thought he spot must surely be a romantic hotspot after sunset, but at this hour, the space was mostly empty. Pamela asked the hostess to seat them in the back near the deck railing that overlooked a tiny river, which quietly wound its way through the town behind a mile of business fronts.

The iron table they sat at was red and its chairs green, reminding Kristen of the scotch-patterned recliner she had found the older woman sitting upon in the retirement home. When Hill eventually requested a Caesar salad from their server without looking at the menu, Kristen followed suit and doubled the order to buy Hill the swift privacy she was after.

"Have you slept in the house?" Hill began, taking a sip of her iced water.

"Valon has visited me," she replied to the point.

Hill looked as if the statement had injured her.

"He's come to me on several occasions."

"Is that why you came to seek me out," Pamela asked in a suspicious tone, "because you know now what he is?"

"What is he, Miz Hill?" Kristen asked evenly.

"He's a demon," she said, her eyes like ice, her voice resolved to speak as plainly as she could.

"How did you know my father died in the bathroom?" Kristen asked, unwilling to address the woman's angry statement.

"Because that's where he attacked the only man I ever brought into that house," said Hill.

"What happened?" Kristen asked.

"I moved into that house after I became a widow. It had been our dream... well, it had been my husband's dream to move to Cambria to retire. Bobby was a senior vice president with Pacific Gas and Electric, and he wanted to retire with his pension and live in a quiet little liberal town on the sea where no one would bother us. He talked about it frequently as if we already lived there—the dream was that clear in his mind."

Kristen didn't move as the woman spoke, not even to nod her head in acknowledgment. Hill's statements had paralyzed her.

"Are you too young to understand what it meant to be a black man in the nineteen-sixties and seventies? Even in the nineteen-eighties, Bobby was unique in his office. Hell, he was a damned unicorn who spent his days in boardrooms surrounded by nothing but white men. You see, though Bobby was more intelligent and gifted than his peers, the company had only promoted him to vice president to satisfy integration laws. They allowed him into those rooms only when legal changes were made to support the civil rights of black Americans. And those men hated Bobby for it. They hated him even more that I was his wife.

"I say all this for you understand how important it was for my husband to make it to Cambria, to make it to retirement. He suffered indignities I still can't bring myself to say aloud. But Bobby walked calmly through them with his head held high. He did it so we could come here when he reached fifty-five and live our life openly and safely.

"So, when he died from a heart attack only two years before he qualified for retirement, I wanted to kill myself. Those miserable bastards gave us nothing. They couldn't even find the decency to attend his funeral. We received a cheap bouquet of white flowers from the company. If it hadn't been for Bobby's insistence on paying the maximum life insurance he could qualify for, I'd still be in San Jose struggling on Social Security.

"After what they did to him, I couldn't stand to let them ruin his dream. So, I took every penny I had and bought the only house in Cambria I could afford—the murder house. I bought it at auction from the state because a young man had been murdered in it a decade earlier. I bought it for Bobby so he could rest knowing that, in the end, we had made our dream come true."

Her memories overcame the woman. She stopped to breathe through the pain as it crippled her face with anguish.

"And then he came back to me," said Hill when she could. "On a day when I didn't know if I truly wanted to live without him anymore—Bobby's spirit came to hold and comfort me. He held me as I grieved for him, and we were together in that house until your parents purchased it from me."

Pamela paused again to stare at Kristen in silence.

"But you know now... it wasn't my Bobby who came to me," Hill whispered.

"It was Valon," said Kristen. "When did you understand?"

"He told me his real name, eventually. I think he was relieved to say it aloud. But I knew for certain he wasn't my husband when I grew to have feelings for another man," she said. "After years of the spirit comforting me, I came to believe I needed to release him—let him go to Heaven where he belonged. I told him I had grown stronger and was ready to carry on with my life. I performed a ceremony in the house, prayed three full rosaries, each word bent on releasing him from his burden. I promised Bobby I would be with him again one day in Heaven and bid him go on to his maker. But he wouldn't leave. That was the first day he let me see his real face.

"At first, I felt ashamed that I had allowed the spirit to hold me in its sway for so many years. I told myself he had defiled the memory of my husband. I grew to become angry with the demon. Still, he treated me only with love.

And, God forgive me, in moments of weakness, I let him continue to make love to me. I allowed him to seduce me free of his pretense, without his disguise.

"But then, life changed for me on its own. I met a man, Alfred, through a mutual friend, and we soon became close. Eventually, we became intimate. It was Alfred's companionship that helped me not to need Valon so desperately. And in those weeks and months, I shunned Valon every time he tried to make love to me. I continued to tell him I wanted him to move on and leave me at peace, but my protests invariably saddened him. He would say to me he loved me and needed me by his side, and the sentiment grew like cinders in my mouth.

"The plan formed in my mind long before I could understand what it might mean, but I was desperate to be rid of the spirit. I had spent many nights with Alfred at his home, telling him I wasn't ready to share my house or my memories with him just yet. Until one night, when I asked Alfred to take me home and invited him inside. When we became intimate in my bedroom, I felt as if I had changed everything. Valon didn't appear, and I enjoyed my night with Alfred. I thought those weeks of rejection had done the trick. But in the middle of the night, Alfred got up to use the bathroom.

"Valon assaulted him?" Kristen asked softly.

"Alfred said very little to me afterward," Pamela answered, "and I never saw him again after that night. But I'll never forget what he said before he left me—that a young man with black hair and blue eyes had appeared in the bathroom, grabbed him by the throat, and attempted to kill him."

Kristen couldn't hide from her father and Ryan's deaths any longer. The woman's description had made disbelief impossible, and Kristen sat back in her seat, incapacitated by the truth she had refused to acknowledge.

"But why my father?" asked Kristen, her voice a mangled whisper of sorrow.

"Because he's a demon," said Hill, her hand trembling as she reached for the glass of water. "Whatever he needed from your father no longer mattered, so he killed him. I'm certain of it."

Hill stopped speaking so she could focus on bringing the glass to her lips. The server returned to the table with their salads, but Kristen's abrupt thanks sent him away without lag.

"I thought about what I should do," continued Hill, "about what I could do to stop it. I considered asking my parish priest for an exorcism, but I knew he couldn't do such a thing. It's not like the old days when people had faith. He would sooner have sent me to the booby hatch to be committed. So, then I thought about destroying the house. We insured it against fire; every home in California must be nowadays. The fire marshal wouldn't question a single woman in her seventies who'd let a grease fire get out of hand."

"What stopped you?" asked Kristen, the woman's idea striking her as the perfect solution.

"I was a coward," Hill answered loudly. "I began to think of all the things in my house—my mementos and photos of Bobby, of our life together. God forgive me, I couldn't do it. I was too cowardly to let them all perish. I might take one or two photos with me, but they would see it was arson if the house were devoid of all those things, the possessions I wouldn't be parted from.

"So, I placed it for sale. I only met your parents one time when they came to negotiate the price, but I couldn't look at them in the eye. As I packed my things, Valon came to me over and over, begging me not to leave him. It was at that point I knew for sure he couldn't follow me, that he was bound to the house. Spirits are, you know. They say many souls are locked to whatever place they died at, that the dead must resolve something from life before they can pass on. Anyhow, when I walked out the front door for the last time, I was rid of him.

"Of course, now I live in a one-room studio apartment that costs five times the price because I need assistance, and all of those things I couldn't bear to live without sit in a storage closet I can't even visit on my own," Hill added.

"My boyfriend died three days ago," said Kristen without emotion. "I found him dead in that bathroom. The coroner said he slipped and hit his head on the bathtub edge, just like my father did."

Pamela received Kristen's statement as if she'd suffered a blow to the face, and she brought her trembling hands to cover her eyes.

"I'm sorry," she wept quietly, her voice gravely wounded by the inescapable truth of her inaction. "I'm so sorry."

CHAPTER FIFTEEN

The ladies fell into silence after Kristen revealed the circumstances of the two "accidents" that took place in her house. The quiet continued after they left the restaurant to drive back to Sunset Villas. It wasn't until the car had stopped in the forecourt of the retirement center, and Pamela was preparing herself to exit Kristen's sedan, that she spoke again.

"You mustn't believe him," said Hill with a tempered resolution in her voice. "I understand why it will be difficult for you to resist, to step away from his power, but you mustn't believe a single thing he says to you."

Pamela opened the car door and gradually stepped up from the passenger seat, steadying herself with the door frame when she was finally on her feet.

"I don't know if you're a person of faith," the woman said weakly, "fewer and fewer young people are. But he's not a man, and he doesn't love you. He's a demon, and a demon is capable of any evil while you feed it with your attention. You've got to get away from there."

Kristen didn't know what to say to the woman, silently holding her gaze.

"God bless you, Kristen," Pamela said finally, then closed the car door behind her to return through the facility's front doors.

As Kristen watched the woman move out of sight, she turned her attention back to the task before her, pulling out of the driveway to head back to Cambria.

Something didn't feel right about any of it, she thought. The anger Kristen had eaten through at lunch now made her nauseous, and it took all her composure to drive the car safely through the small town of San Luis Obispo. Her every thought circled the feeling of certainty Pamela had given her. There was no doubt in Kristen's mind that Valon had murdered her father. Kristen felt the truth echo through her every attempt to analyze the facts in her possession.

Still, Kristen continued to look for other answers. The psychologist had been well-trained to analyze a puzzle from every conceivable viewpoint. Long before Kristen's formal education, it was a method for thinking her father had insisted upon from his daughter. Whenever she was angry or jealous or impatient or saddened by anything, Richard Cole asked Kristen to explain to him why it might be possible her emotion was mistaken. It was an exercise in logic that required empathy when it was the very last skill she felt capable of at the moment, and it regularly infuriated the child. That fury threatened to break Kristen now while she attempted to break through each wall guarding Hill's inescapable truth: Valon had murdered Kristen's father, just as he had murdered Ryan. Whatever Valon was, be it a demon, as Pamela insisted, or merely the spirit of a man attached to the house, Kristen was confident of one thing, and all the analysis in the world wouldn't change her mind.

Valon was a murderer.

At the last red light before entering the 101 Freeway, Kristen reached in her bag to grab her phone, finding a message waiting for her when the device's screen lit up. Starting the playback over the car speakers before the turn toward the on-ramp opened, Kristen listened to her supervisor at Sharp Medical confirm a one-month leave of absence had been granted. The man repeated the news twice that they expected the psychologist to confirm her return to work at least five days before the period ended. It was the last thing Kristen gave a damn about now, but it was still one less practical thing with which she needed to concern herself.

When she arrived home, Kristen found Tony seated in the backyard on a patio chair, eating his lunch and listening to music on a small Bluetooth speaker. Penelope sat beside Tony but jolted when she smelled her mother at the gate, the sound of her human's approach masked by the violence of Parkway Drive's raging vocals.

"Everything going okay?" she asked when the young man lowered his music.

"It's going well," Tony said, his eyes pleased to see Kristen up and about. "What time would you like to head for the showers?"

"How about in an hour?" Kristen proposed.

"Sounds good," Tony answered, raising his thermos of water in a silent toast to the deal.

There was something about Tony's smile that helped Kristen feel a sense of normalcy, despite the complications between them and the horrors engulfing her life. In truth, Kristen's former problems with Tony meant less than nothing to her now, and his smile continued to warm her broken heart each time he flashed it. He and Penelope now remained the one thing Kristen could rely upon for a sense of stability, which meant everything in this place filled with anything but.

The quiet of the house assaulted Kristen when she walked inside and shut the door. Feelings that betrayed the surrounding peace overwhelmed her. In her room, Kristen considered attempting a nap—just a short one that might open the door to another visit. But Kristen couldn't have slept now if she downed a bottle of NyQuil. The adrenalin was still seething through her veins, a crippling dose of liquid anger, the resulting rage searching for something to throw.

"Valon!" Kristen finally yelled at the walls, only to hear the silence of the house around her.

When she screamed his name again, the answer that came was the melodic marimba of her cell phone ringer. Reaching in her bag, she found an unprogrammed number calling. Kristen was inclined to chuck the phone back at her bag but stopped when she recognized the area code was local.

"This is Doctor Cole," Kristen announced after she tapped the green button to connect the call.

"Hello, am I speaking with Kristen Cole?"

"This is she," Kristen said again, with even less patience.

"Good afternoon, this is Sheriff Johnson from the San Luis Obispo Sheriff's Office. I'm calling to inform you that our department has completed its investigation into the death of Ryan Hoffman."

"Yes?" Kristen asked promptly during the break in the man's words, which was nothing more than him taking a breath.

"The department will not bring charges at this time. As such, you may schedule a bio-mediation team to clean up the affected areas within your home. I'm happy to refer you to a reputable company in the area. I can even transfer you to them if you want."

"Yes, thank you," said Kristen as her voice tempered. "I would appreciate being transferred."

"Very well, Miz Cole," Johnson said. "Please hold."

When the transferred line eventually came on, a female receptionist answered and informed Kristen she had received the go-ahead from the Sheriff's Office to schedule service. The receptionist quoted her a time and price estimate to complete their services. It was no minor pleasure for Kristen to be told they were available for an early morning appointment the next day.

When she'd ended the call, Kristen no longer had the urge to chuck the heavy iPhone back at her bag. Instead, she laid it down gently and exhaled. Kristen felt a strong sense of relief, coupled with the need to tell Tony the news. One of a dozen pressure points praying upon the woman's mind was that the young man had been so unfairly inconvenienced by an ordeal that had nothing to do with him. Kristen made her way back through the house to find him at once.

On her way, Kristen stopped in her tracks when she came upon the staircase, seeing the black and yellow 'Do Not Cross' sheriff's tape guarding the way up. As if the previous moments hadn't happened, Kristen became over-whelmed by rage again. She felt white-hot rage for what had happened to her father, to Ryan, to Tony, to all of them.

Kristen pulled the strands of tape aside, letting them flutter weightlessly down against the banister, and impa-tiently stomped upstairs. Her heavy footfalls shook the frame of the house, evoking cracks of objection from the wooden steps. Arriving on the landing, Kristen looked down the hallway to the master bedroom door, seeing the sheriffs had also taped it closed. She continued her advance past the other upstairs doors to rip down the obstacle.

Opening the master bedroom door, Kristen pushed in to find the space just as she'd left it days ago. The bedsheets were in a tangled mess on the ground. There were marks left by the police on the headboard that Kristen didn't recognize.

"Valon!" she screamed at the room. "Show yourself, damn you!"

Kristen moved about the room wildly, looking at every corner to find him, as if he might hide from her behind a chair or window drape.

"You miserable coward, show yourself! Did you do it?! Did you do it to them?! *Demon!*"

Kristen's legs began to tremble violently as fear overtook her frame in the silence that met the echo of her voice.

From the rear of the house just below the room, Kristen heard Penelope bark ferociously, and soon she heard the yard gate shut loudly.

Kristen's eyes turned to the bathroom door, also blocked by a single strand of police tape. She felt terror for what she would find there, but the psychologist refused to let fear stop her hand as it reached for the doorknob.

From downstairs, she heard the front door open and the concerned roar of Tony's voice calling her name.

Deigning to answer, Kristen turned the knob and pushed the dark oak bathroom door open without disturbing the 'Do Not Cross' tape. The door hit the interior wall with a loud thud.

Before Kristen's eyes could register the sight, Kristen smelled it. A wave of rotting urine overwhelmed Kristen's senses, forcing the woman to wince and draw her hand to her face. Dried blood lay where Ryan's head wound had bled out, having encircled his upper body to create a general silhouette of his upper torso.

"Kristen!" Tony yelled from the hallway.

His voice startled her, and Kristen turned away from the bathroom doorframe. Started away from terrifying sight, her legs gave out, and the woman fell loudly to her knees. She screamed at the impact but didn't feel the slightest pain.

Tony entered the room and knelt quickly to help her up. Instead, Kristen reached manically to place her arms around him, securing Tony to her as she buried her face in his chest. Deep sobs wretched through Kristen as Tony's arms instinctively moved to hold her. Into him, the woman released screams of wounded anguish.

CHAPTER SIXTEEN

Tony waited patiently for Kristen to recover from the trauma. Disheartened by her loss of emotional control, he felt obliged to hold the suffering woman for a good while before attempting to move them out of the room. When Kristen's trembling slowed, and the sobs in her chest allowed her to breathe comfortably, Tony whispered tenderly in her ear.

"Let me take you downstairs. You're not ready to be in here."

Kristen didn't respond for some time before she moved her limbs slowly, allowing Tony to slip his arm around her waist and get her up on her feet.

After they'd made their way to the guest room, Tony sat them both down on the air mattress, maintaining the embrace between them.

"Now, why ever did you do that to yourself?" he asked her without a hint of disapproval. "You know we're not supposed to be up there."

Kristen only breathed in response at first, tempering herself in time and wiping the tears from her eyes.

"I had to see it," she whispered with remnants of

unstable gasps darkening her words. "They called me and told me it's over. They won't be investigating us anymore, and someone is coming tomorrow to clean it up. And I just had to look."

Kristen fell back to whimpered sobs, the wave of anguish cresting again for minutes before she could proceed. Tony said nothing, allowing the woman to continue in her own time.

"I'm sorry," Kristen said when she could speak. "I'm sorry I went in there. I'm sorry I did that to you."

"Don't worry about me," Tony replied. "All that matters now is that it's done, and you will be okay."

It occurred to the young man he was whispering words of comfort to the last person he'd expect would need them. This was her job, wasn't it—telling sad people everything would be fine? In fact, Tony believed the woman likely considered his words to be cliched, even an imposition. But then Kristen's body enfolded into him as if he'd said what she needed to hear.

Tony reciprocated the squeeze of Kristen's affection, and when she was ready to lift her head, he moved to kiss her wet cheek tenderly. It felt miserable to watch her suffer. Tony no longer felt the wounded resentment he once harbored for Kristen's actions, taking Hoffman to her bed, and all the young man could think of was how deeply he cared for her.

After his kiss, Tony distinctly felt Kristen harden. Her limbs became less pliant. Her back stiffened, reinforcing the erect posture she'd abandoned during her despair. And at last, Kristen pulled her hand from his to wipe away her tears.

"Thank you," Kristen finally replied. "I don't think they'll bother us any longer."

"That's a relief, I guess," Tony replied. "So, they understand it was all a terrible mistake, just like you told them?"

"There's a company coming tomorrow morning to do a cleanup of the room," Kristen said instead of answering his question. "Would you bring down the packed boxes this afternoon before you leave? It'll be better if everything is out of their way. And I won't be going back into that room."

"Sure thing," said Tony.

He moved to hug her one more time before standing and distinctly felt Kristen's rigidity to his touch. Unprepared to address her change or his fresh embarrassment, Tony left Kristen in the room and ventured back upstairs.

I guess she'll never let me get close to her, the young man resigned bitterly. The sentiment offered Tony a fresh sting, but this was no time to pretend Kristen would ever be anything but what she insisted she was—not his.

There were six packing boxes taped and ready for transport waiting in the master bedroom. Tony started by first moving them out of the space and into the hallway so he could close the bedroom door. He didn't feel right being in the space, regardless of the events he'd shared with Kristen on that bed. After she had carried on without Tony, he would rather not be in there at all, and the clicking sound of the doorknob as it closed carried more symbolic weight for the young man than he cared to admit.

When Tony finally brought the boxes downstairs and into the guest room, he paused as if to imply he'd gladly remain with Kristen. However, she gave him nothing more than quiet words of gratitude, keeping her eyes on her tablet.

"Is there anything else I can get for you?" Tony asked her.

"That's all," she said with an emotionless tone. "I just need to take it easy."

When Tony didn't move from his spot, Kristen eventually pulled her eyes away from the screen and looked up at him.

"Thank you," she told him again.

The words held not the slightest tone of dismissal, but they caused Tony to exhale more sharply than he intended to, receiving them as just that. With a quick nod of his head, he left the room and passed over the threshold without bothering to close the door.

Tony was fucking pissed, more so than he'd ever admitted to himself before. After spending those minutes with Kristen in his arms, Tony was sure there was something greater between them. It was a feeling he'd believed was real for some time, and to end their encounter with another cold shoulder from the woman was too bitter a pill to swallow silently.

Unable to focus, Tony paced through the house aimlessly. His eyes wandered at the spaces before him, but the young man was lost in thought. He again felt the sting of humility, and with it came yet another bout of embarrassment. He felt stupid to have exposed himself again, that he'd allowed Kristen to see how much she meant to him.

What happened between them had been nothing more than a couple of fucks. Kristen had said as much. And they hadn't stopped the woman from continuing without the slightest deference to Tony's feelings. The miserable bitch had walked her latest suitor through the door as Tony worked in the house. She'd even forced him to converse with the man.

Even within the sting of his anger, Tony understood he had only himself to blame for the situation. Kristen had assured him there wouldn't be anything more between them. And even if her actions hinted at more, what the hell made Tony think it was a good idea—allowing her to fill his thoughts for even a moment longer? Kristen had played the big sister, but wasn't that just her allowing the awkwardness of their situation to be livable? And again, she silently promised there would be nothing more between them.

He needed to get her out of his head. He understood the process well enough: a tight shirt and a smile were all it took. After a single drink and ten minutes of agreeable banter, a girl would let him escort her to a bed he'd never see again. It was a simple enough thing to do, but Tony doubted he'd ever feel comfortable picking up a woman at a bar or club.

Tony's brothers never failed to take the piss out of him over how simple it was for him to score.

"Of course, he doesn't have to try," they'd declare. "Can you imagine if the dumb fuck had to put two syllables together to score some pussy? Game over. He should thank God every day for his looks."

But Tony's reluctance to pick up a date in a bar wasn't the result of insecurity over what to say to women. He was insecure about his body, a truth he refused to admit. Not his physique; Tony was comfortable with his athletic shape. Unspoken concerns with his triceps on this day or with his calves on the next required only time in the gym spent to improve them. Instead, Tony's true insecurity was his penis.

It wasn't a matter he could speak to anyone about. As a boy, he'd endured the slings and arrows of his older brothers because all they ever did was make fun of him. In time, Tony found that dropping his shorts to lord his appendage, significantly larger than their own, was a reliable way to interrupt their teasing mid-sentence. Instead, Tony feared bedding a woman because it often ended in disaster.

His first girlfriend had seemed so excited when she'd learned Tony had a large penis. One day in tenth grade, while walking Cathy across campus to their fifth-period class, the young couple came across one of Tony's brothers. Eric said something stupid to goad him. Such communication was a daily hazard when you had older brothers who needed to find any opportunity to make themselves feel better about their faults.

"She must know about your giant dick," he'd blurted when Tony offered the slightest resistance to Eric's barbs. "She's obviously not with you because your dumb ass can color inside the lines."

Tony offered a resigned smile and told Eric to shut his whore's mouth, then took the girl's hand firmly to lead her away from the scene. The fifteen-year-old apologized for his brother's crudeness, but when he'd seen Cathy blush at Eric's comment, Tony felt lionized more than embarrassed.

During that class, Cathy pretended to have forgotten her textbook, a simple ploy to be closer to Tony, as the teacher allowed her to slide her desk over to share. After barely a paragraph into the day's review of the American Civil War, Tony felt Cathy's hand reach discreetly under the desk. She boldly slid her fingers over his crotch, finding the large bulge of flesh in his jeans. Tony's cock instantly stirred. He shifted in his seat and sat back to adjust himself as it grew and pushed awkwardly against the unforgiving fabric. When Cathy felt the organ stiffen, she smiled as if the response was marvelous. She ran her fingers mercilessly along the shaft until it reached uncomfortably past his waist toward her.

Tony had loved every minute of that class.

That event had led to others, as Cathy found any excuse to sit near him and tease his cock to attention. She unashamedly reveled in this power, exerting it frequently over Tony and her new toy. In science class, under a large shared table, Cathy boldly reached inside his jeans and underwear to pull his penis out and expose him. The feel of her skin rubbing against his cock was as thrilling as its exposure to light proved concerning. When he'd stopped her, anxiously looking around them to find who might have noticed, Cathy took his hand and guided it to rest between her legs. It was a simple gesture of acknowledgment on the girl's part—Tony had rightfully earned the privilege to touch her most private place.

He was mad for Cathy, and they soon seized upon an opportunity to have sex at her girlfriend's house one weekend. It was there that Tony first learned the truth about himself.

It started with frustration, then pain, then tears, and finally, sadness. The two were incompatible, and all their attempts that afternoon resulted in the same conclusion.

Cathy might not have realized how mortified the experience had left Tony, as she was so embarrassed and pained by her inability to accommodate him. The look of fear in her eyes had only increased with each failed attempt. The next day, she ended their relationship over the phone. The rejection affected Tony so wholly it took him years to muster the courage to try sex again.

His second partner was only a little better-suited to accommodate him, and his third partner offered a flat-out rejection the moment she came face-to-face with his intimidating organ. The trial and failure became a debilitating pattern for the boy, following him into manhood.

Women might loudly vocalize their opinion on the

matter before he drummed up the courage to ask them to bed. So many seemed thrilled by the idea of fucking a guy with a big cock, even demanding it, until that moment when they realized what it truly meant.

The mechanics of most women's bodies ensured that Tony's organ would push uncomfortably against their cervix before he'd get the change to begin the act in earnest. If he restrained himself from entering her more than halfway, Tony still had to tolerate the incomplete sensation while the woman invariably grit her teeth to accommodate the pain of his girth.

That scenario only changed once when Tony was twenty-two and found the perfect partner. She was an older woman, almost twice his age, who seemed to be designed specifically for him. It was the first time Tony had experienced sex as something glorious, instead of an exercise in urgent disappointment and shame. In time, this perfect arrangement revealed itself for what it was: a married woman stepping out on her husband. It quietly bothered Tony, even if it didn't matter to the woman. But in time, she broke off the relationship. When Tony soon found himself with another woman, again confronted by the incompatibility of normality, he avoided sex altogether after that.

That is until Kristen Cole came into his life.

She'd dragged the frenzy out of him again. More importantly, Kristen had been able to accommodate Tony. Maybe not as well as his perfect housewife, but well enough that he'd been able to enjoy sex again.

It was an unexpected gift, but one taken from him almost immediately. And now, as Tony again faced the truth that Kristen was yet one more woman not meant for him, the bitterness seethed painfully through the young man's veins.

Standing in the living room, Tony tripped on a small stub of wood scrap left over by mistake. He reached for it and cast it violently into the nearby trash can. The resulting hollow bang was far louder than he expected, and Tony struggled to regain control of his emotions before his embarrassment amplified them.

Examining the source of the bang, he saw a box lying within the can. Tony reached down and pulled out a Ouija board game, the last thing he expected to find.

Kristen must have placed it there. Had she tried to commune with the dead—with her father or Ryan?

The implications hit Tony in the gut, and this time it was his insensitivity that humiliated him. Tony had worked himself into a frenzy of pathetic self-pity, even as the girl was clearly suffering. He felt disgusted by his earlier thoughts, and a different weight took over his self-indignation—Tony was ashamed of himself.

From his pants pocket, he felt his cell phone vibrate.

"This is Tony," he answered heavily.

"Yeah, hello there, Tony. This is Andrew Kim."

"Oh, hey," he answered, baffled to hear the man's voice again.

"Listen," Kim began, "I just talked to the client at the job lined up next, and they need to push back a couple of weeks. So, if you're serious about moving forward quickly, if you have the money ready, I can begin the work there as early as the day after tomorrow."

"Wow, yeah," Tony replied. "I'm ready for you."

"Have you resolved that problem upstairs?" the man asked, a slight wariness coloring his voice.

"It has," Tony confirmed. "The hallway bathroom is wide open for you."

"Alright, fine," Kim conceded. "From the condition of the wall piping that extends up through to the second floor, I'm guessing I need to review the upstairs before I can offer you a solid bid."

Tony felt another pang of defeat building.

"But if it's identical, as you say, I'll go on the presumption that it requires the same work, plus the floor extension. I'll send you over a preliminary estimate in an hour or so. There doesn't seem to be as much there to do as I expected.

"That sounds excellent," said Tony with a swelling heart.

"The upstairs bath is similarly demolitioned, correct?" asked Kim.

"It is," confirmed Tony. "Would you like me to shoot you over some pictures?"

"Sure, that'll help."

"You got it," Tony said and smiled at the empty room before him.

The two men exchanged a couple of pleasantries before ending the call, and Tony lifted the phone in silent triumph at his luck. He walked back through the downstairs to the guest room, excited to let Kristen know they had overcome another hurdle.

Arriving at the room, Tony found that Kristen had lain down and gone to sleep. He quieted himself, awkwardly aware of the noise he'd made in entering the room. From the mattress, Kristen jolted awake as if she hadn't meant to close her eyes.

"I'm so sorry," Tony sucked his teeth.

"No, it's okay, I'm just so tired," she mumbled.

"Of course," said Tony. "Listen, I'm gonna head out in a few and do some prep back at the shop. Do you want me to let Penny in for you? She's probably missing you after what happened earlier."

"Yeah, would you?" she asked.

"Sure," he answered.

Realizing that he still held the Ouija board game in his left hand, Tony placed it quietly on top of the stacked boxes in the room before moving to let the Husky inside.

"Go see Mommy," he told Penny, and watched the dog move briskly through the bottom floor to attend to her human.

After he'd shot a couple photos of the upstairs hall bathroom, Tony messaged them to Kim and received a quick thumbs-up emoji from the plumber. Satisfied, the young man packed up and left for home.

CHAPTER SEVENTEEN

V alon noticed Margaret Cole that first night she
slept under his roof. The noise and discord of
the previous month, when Pamela left him, had
swelled Valon with such pain and resentment, he had
closed himself off altogether from the sound of change. If
a threat did arise, something Valon must attend to, he
knew his faceless master would pull him to attention.

But while no danger came, the smell of death woke
Valon. He could sense it, the parasite that grew within
this new woman now living in the house. Valon had never
confronted its unique presence, and it captured his attention such that he was forced back into consciousness, the
last thing he wanted. Even Pamela's anger and dark bitterness never released such a unique fragrance. This other
woman was being eaten alive, and she did not seem to
know it.

Valon entered her thoughts when she dreamed, during
those moments when her mind's defenses rested and were
most susceptible to his observation. Margaret dreamt of
many things that first night: playing as a child and fighting
with the girls across the street. Then the dream shifted to

the narrative of a television show, some disagreement between two lovers on a soap opera. Margaret inhabited the role of the scorned woman, enduring the pain of humiliation and rejection when the son of a bitch betrayed her. She obsessed over how to get even for what he'd done. And finally, the melancholy of disappointment opened the door to another memory, one which Valon could tell was a real experience through which the woman had once suffered.

Margaret was little more than a child. In fact, she had just turned eighteen and had begun her first semester at The University of California, Los Angeles. It terrified the girl to be there; she didn't know a soul. It hadn't been her idea to come to this place, but the oppressive expectation of her parents. Unlike Margaret's much older sister, Ruby Jean, college was not something that aroused her enthusiasm. Margaret wanted to marry because she wanted a husband to take care of her. Ruby Jean had gone on and on about how important it was to have an education, to prepare yourself for a competitive world. But the woman's logic always sounded like nonsense to Margaret—modern propaganda for unattractive women to intimidate others. The girl knew only too well that the finest women in the community of Pasadena were wives. What woman could own a house west of the Brookside Golf Course by herself? An heiress, perhaps. Otherwise, those homes were the property of physicians, film producers, politicians, and attorneys—the men who ran Los Angeles.

If she must spend the next four years in this place, Margaret would damn well be sure to find herself on the arm of a future doctor. But today, she was by herself in search of an English literature class that would begin in seconds.

When Margaret's eyes read 'Room 206' on the sign

affixed to the dark oak door, she ran smack into a young man with a chest like a wall. The collision bumped her so hard that Margaret fell backward on her rear, causing the books she carried to crash to the surrounding floor.

In her shock, Margaret looked up to see the young man staring down in confusion from his towering height.

"Darn it, I'm sorry," he said, before kneeling to reach for her hand.

When Margaret made it to her feet, the handsome boy knelt again to gather her books as swiftly as he could.

"Are you all right?" he asked, pushing back a forelock of the silky dark hair that fell in his eyes.

"I think so," Margaret answered, reaching to adjust her blonde curls, ensuring they hadn't fallen apart.

"I'm awful sorry—that was my fault," he told her with his deep voice. "Where are you headed?"

"I need to get into that classroom there," she pointed to the door only five feet away.

The young man turned and reached for the door handle and pulled it open with a smile, extending his hand to invite her in.

"Thank you," Margaret answered him with a blushing smile and proceeded through the threshold, turning back to look at the chivalrous young man before the oak door closed between them.

And in two hours, when the miserable class had concluded, Margaret found the dashing young man waiting for her in the hall where she'd left him. The sight of his dreamy eyes beaming at her when she entered the hallway startled Margaret, and she stopped walking without meaning to.

"How was your class?" he asked with a cocky smile.

"Dreadful," she answered, fighting the urge to laugh.

The simple act of surprising her positively sent

Margaret to the moon. An erotic attraction overcame the girl, and a scalding color filled her cheeks. The young man was exquisite, so tall and broad-shouldered, and the whole of these sensations made her slightly dizzy.

"I didn't get the chance to introduce myself before you got away from me," he smirked as if enjoying the effect his stunt had achieved. "My name is Chris Jackson."

And that was the moment that stayed with Margaret forever. She thought of it frequently whenever the slightest event prompted her to remember the sensation of young love. Chris Jackson became the embodiment of everything about love that held fresh and exciting to her.

In the days after Jackson introduced himself, Margaret became infatuated by the dazzling young man. Even if he hadn't been studying pre-law, she would have gladly forgotten any notion of her quest to find a rich future husband to be with him. Margaret became obsessed with Chris: the warmth of his large hand when he held hers, the confident smirk he shot back when she attempted to land a joke, the light in his eyes when they spoke of the latest film they'd seen, and the deep bass of his voice when the boy whispered how he loved her.

It was all there, these moments of perfect joy. They composed the very framework of her memories, each filled with its individual flavor of ideal bliss. These memories played again and again during the dream before Valon detected a dark well of pain overshadow them.

The day came when Margaret saw Chris smiling in the distance as he sat on a bench in Dickson Court. Beside him sat another girl who shyly giggled when he bent in to kiss her cheek. As powerful as Margaret's first memory of Chris had been, she now experienced its inverse as adrenaline rushed through her veins. The chemical poisoned her with its sharp blade, threatening to slice into her soul.

That had been the end for the girl, the last moment she ever allowed herself to feel love in that way; wholly with such blind trust. And by the time she'd been ready to let the next boy take her out on a date, the door to Margaret's soul had firmly closed. In time, the young woman found someone she cared for, someone financially successful who would take care of her, but it was never the same as it had been during those first months in Chris' arms.

The darkness of Margaret's resolve shocked Valon, and he reached out to stop the dream from descending into anguish and bitterness. He coaxed her thoughts back, scene by scene, slowing her raging heartbeat until she stood again in the hallway with Chris. Valon picked this moment to walk right into the boy's body and stare out at Margaret's crystal blue eyes.

He thought her so beautiful, the scarlet flooding her high cheeks serving to make her even more lovely.

"I can't believe you waited for me," Margaret said, her white smile breaking through any semblance of self-control left to the girl.

"Can I buy you a soda?" Valon asked. "There's a cafeteria just down the path away."

Margaret looked down at the floor as if wholly unprepared for this moment.

"Sure," she answered, and smiled again when her eyes returned to meet his gaze.

Valon extended his arm to let the young girl take it shyly, then led her through the building and out into the warm sunshine.

"So, what is your name?" he smirked with his deep voice.

"I'm Maggie," she answered.

CHAPTER EIGHTEEN

Valon returned to Margaret Cole night after night that first month as she slept in his house. In each instance, he guided her back to those precious memories of Chris Jackson.

At first, she resisted Valon's pull toward the specific memories he wanted to see, the ones that promised to excite and gratify him. The challenge was that Margaret preferred the simple moments between them, like how it felt to hold Chris' arm when he led her to his shining red Buick Skylark. When Jackson opened the passenger door for her, the young woman smiled with a satisfaction that bordered upon ecstasy, one that often outshone her sexual memories. From Margaret's recall, Valon understood Jackson was everything she had ever dreamed of. He wasn't the crude, drunken slob that Margaret's father had been. Instead, Chris was a prince among men who treated her how she'd always wanted. Margaret fancied herself to be upon the arm of a celebrity. He was a young Rock Hudson or Montgomery Clift. He was like Elvis, a living god whose flawless smile gleamed from the posters papered over the walls of her older sister's bedroom. And he was Margaret's alone.

That Chris Jackson came from money and lavished it upon her was merely the icing on the cake. He took Margaret to several glamorous restaurants in Los Angeles, where he tipped the host to seat them at the finest table, usually dead center in the room where everyone could see them. Chris often hinted at his desire for intimacy, but he never pushed her. He was a gentleman, and this simple fact made Margaret more physically attracted to him than she could bear.

In time, Valon succeeded in guiding Margaret to that first night when she'd allowed Chris to take her to the Roosevelt Hotel in Hollywood. They dined in the lobby restaurant surrounded by the most beautiful people she'd ever set her eyes on. After the waiter cleared dessert, Margaret shocked the boy by asking him to get a room for them. Chris had been only too agreeable to the request, and they soon ascended the hotel's many floors inside its stylish golden elevator.

"I'll just be a short while," she said as they arrived in the room, and slipped into the small bathroom.

While the door was closed behind her, Margaret promptly used the toilet, then washed her hands and checked herself in the mirror. She reapplied her lipstick and added a little powder to reduce the shine on her nose. Margaret looked perfect for him, and she couldn't help let out a small bit of laughter at herself.

How marvelous this all is, she thought. Margaret's mother had stressed more than once that she really ought to wait to engage in sex with her husband. But the intrepid woman was a pragmatist and had done her best to send her daughter to college with everything she needed, including "the talk." The woman's descriptions had been unsatisfactory, but Margaret gleaned from them one certainty: it would hurt.

But the girl didn't care about that tonight. Margaret was so attracted to Chris that she would endure any discomfort to please him. And in this famous hotel of all places.

Running her slight hands through her blonde hair, teasing it out to appear wild like Marilyn Monroe, Margaret couldn't think of a single reason she shouldn't have sex with Chris. If she didn't intend for him to enjoy undressing her, the girl would have walked back into that bedroom stark naked.

When she finally reemerged, Margaret heard jazz music coming from the clock radio by the bed. Chris had already removed his jacket and red silk tie. He had unbuttoned his white shirt down to mid-chest. The sight stimulated Margaret such that she forgot to breathe for several heartbeats.

"You're so beautiful," he whispered and drew the girl to him.

In his arms, Margaret received Jackson's warm kiss without resistance. She felt the urgency build in him, but even when his kiss became wet, the girl did nothing to stop him from having his way with her. His hands were everywhere, and in time Margaret felt him pull gently at the zipper back of her dress. Jackson pulled the garment down to expose her neck and shoulders, then changed his attention to her brassiere.

Margaret's heart raced at the sublime sensation of being under his control. Only her certainty that Chris was just as excited as she outweighed it. The boy's breath came so densely now that when he kissed her neck, Margaret giggled at the sensation. Her cocktail dress fell to the floor, threatening Margaret's exposed flesh to take on a slight chill. But she felt nothing but the pleasure of his attention.

Chris pulled at the straps of her white satin bra. Sensing he didn't know how to unhook it, Margaret reached back to unfasten it for him. The man's response as the garment fell away from her breasts was the most exciting thing that ever happened to the girl. Jackson became incensed by the exposed flesh before him, the hardened nipples standing with proud defiance, and he urgently lifted them to his mouth to lavish the wet adoration they deserved.

"I love you," she whispered, holding Jackson by the back of his head to her chest.

The boy pulled away at Margaret's words and kissed her lips again.

"Come here," said Chris, and drew Margaret by her hand to the large bed.

He ripped off the coverlet and laid Margaret down on the crisp white linen, then reached under her bottom to pull off her satin underwear. This new sensation of exposure was more than Margaret was prepared for, though it was hypothetically what she wanted. The feel of being naked and on her back, however, filled the girl with an unexpected apprehension. When Jackson paused and stared down at Margaret with such intense scrutiny, she moved to cover her breasts and close her legs to hide.

The insecure nature of her shame seemed to drive Jackson wild for Margaret, and he reached to pull her legs apart to expose her sex again. The boy did this without request, and she struggled to keep from reaching to cover herself when Chris kissed her there. The move shocked the girl. Though it was the most sublime sensation, Margaret realized she wasn't at all prepared to experience it. Her mother had never even hinted at such an act, and

Margaret felt her mind swim as she submitted to Jackson's invasions.

When he'd seemed to have his fill of this unmentionable act, Chris lifted himself back to his feet at the foot of the bed and undressed. Margaret caught her breath to see him standing there, his cock fully erect, standing solidly at attention. The girl had seen her father's body a few times, and she knew what a penis looked like, but she'd never seen it in this state. Her mother's description of "stiffening" was a moronic disservice to the girl, she now realized.

Jackson fell gently between her legs, and he situated himself to begin. Margaret gritted her teeth in anticipation of the pain several seconds before he even positioned his organ to enter her.

"Relax, Maggie," he whispered. "I'll be a gentle as I can."

"Thank you," she breathed honestly and relaxed her sex as he stroked the head of his cock upon and down along it. The gentle, rhythmic touch helped her to ease as much as she could.

When he rested his cock against her opening, he brought the weight of his body down on Margaret and lowered his head to whisper in her ear.

"Don't worry, Maggie. You'll be fine—I promise. Just breathe and relax," Jackson said.

Before she could respond with words or loosen her body further, Margaret felt Jackson's lips on her earlobe, which he sucked into his mouth. To her surprise, Margaret felt Jackson's teeth bite down barely a second before he pushed his cock inside of her, causing a sharp pain in both locations. In confusion, Margaret yelled out uncontrollably.

KRISTEN'S EYES opened to the darkness of the room. The streaking images of her dream continued to mingle against the absence of light in the room. Her heart pounded in her chest in concert with her deep breaths. Kristen had reached between her legs to fend off the pain she endured in the dream. It had all been so real that Kristen was hesitant to let herself go until she was sure the pain was not there.

From beside her, Kristen heard Penelope growl.

"I'm sorry, sweetheart," she said to the Husky. "It's okay."

Kristen reached beside her and felt her dog's soft coat, petting it gently to reassure her.

"I'm okay, sweetie. Mommy's okay."

Penelope's growling didn't stop. Kristen could feel the vibration from the animal's deep timbre and immediately became alarmed. Kristen wondered if the animal might become dangerous and bite her. It was the last thing she would've expected, but Kristen withdrew her hand and reached for her iPhone lying on the floor beside the air mattress.

She tapped to engage the camera's flash and lit up the room, pointing the small LED up at the ceiling.

"Penelope," Kristen whispered gently, "it's okay."

In the dim light, the Husky's face became apparent as she cast her bright blue eyes intensely at the wall behind Kristen's head.

The woman turned her gaze for only a moment before sitting up and turning back to get a good look at the wall. Kristen expected to find that an insect had caused the dog's protective response. At least, she hoped it was a bug and not a spider. With Cambria's wealth of towering pine trees, the region was a favorite for tarantulas. They were the massive furry variety, and the mere thought of them set Kristen's flesh to prickle at attention.

Dissatisfied that she couldn't see whatever miserable intruder was on the wall, Kristen stood up from the mattress and walked across the room to flick the light switch, illuminating the two wall sconces. Her eyes squinted at the bright influx of light, but in a moment, she could focus her gaze on the wall where Penelope continued to growl.

Nothing.

Kristen looked methodically at the small space, unable to find a single furry leg or antenna. She walked around the mattress and stood behind Penelope, looking directly to where the animal's nose pointed.

The dog lifted herself slowly to her paws and adopted a threatening posture, her ears pulled back, head bowed in position to strike. The growl in her chest rumbled ferociously.

Kristen was too shocked to move, much less speak to comfort or scold the animal. She could only watch in confused silence.

Penelope released a single earsplitting bark that sent every hair on Kristen's body to stand up. Both the animal and whatever she meant to attack now terrified the woman. She soon forced herself to breathe, remembering what Tony had told her the other day.

Kristen knew for sure now—she had rodents in her walls.

CHAPTER NINETEEN

Tony arrived at half-past seven to make sure he was present for Kristen's cleaning crew. Penny ran to Tony the moment he opened the front door and rose on her hind legs to deliver a volley of kisses to his cheek.

"She missed you last night," said Kristen, who surprised Tony by being both up and dressed for the day.

"How's that?" he asked, more to the Husky than her owner.

"I woke from a nightmare in the middle of the night, and I opened my eyes to find her growling at the walls," said Kristen. "She scared the shit out of me. She was so intense about it. I would've sworn we were in danger."

Tony adopted a defeated expression and gave the dog's coat one last scratch before gently pushing her paws off his chest and back to the ground.

"Once upon a time, you might've been," he remarked. "They attributed the Black Plague, in part, to the spreading of the virus by rodents. Perhaps Penny's ancestors still speak through her DNA."

"They felt strongly about the matter last night. Did you hear from the exterminator?" Kristen asked.

"I did, and they will be here today sometime between noon and six," Tony answered. "But that's only to inspect and determine something we're now certain of. I couldn't guess when the company will be available to do the actual work needed to get rid of the problem, or what it's all going to cost."

"Their window of arrival is six hours long?" she squinted.

"It's a decent job," he answered, raising his coffee cup in a mock toast. "Like water and power, exterminators haven't any need to be accountable for great customer service. There will always be pests in need of disposal."

"I guess so," Kristen said and raised her eyebrows.

"Is the cleanup crew still coming at eight this morning?" Tony inquired.

"Allegedly," Kristen answered with a vacant nod.

"How are you feeling?" he asked, lowering his voice to an intimate register.

Kristen exhaled slowly and offered no other answer for some time. Even then, her voice seemed to bear so much pain that Tony regretted asking his question. Not because he didn't care to know the answer, but because he did.

"I'm not doing well," she finally said with defeat. "I'm at a crossroads, and I feel myself moving towards the path I know is a mistake."

"Why go that way then?" Tony asked, mildly.

Kristen shook her head, seeming to be at a loss. "It's something so compelling that I can't help myself. I have to know for sure it's a mistake."

Tony smiled gradually, not knowing how to respond to such a simple answer from the woman, who he estimated to be miles smarter than himself.

"What would seal the deal?" he countered. "What would have to happen for you to know a mistake is a mistake?"

Kristen looked at Tony with terrified eyes.

"I've learned something about this place that's changed everything for me," she said. "I've had experiences I can't explain or discredit. No, that's not true—I can explain them. But I don't believe in my explanations anymore. These aren't delusions I'm experiencing. This isn't schizophrenia. Schizophrenics don't share delusions this precisely with strangers."

It was Tony's turn to stare at Kristen with grave concern. He didn't know much about schizophrenia, short of television shows or jokes made about people who had it. Tony understood it was something crazy people had when they saw things or heard voices that weren't there. The homeless woman who walked past him having elaborate conversations with someone who wasn't there—she had schizophrenia. To see an exceptional woman like Kristen, a doctor of all people, say the word and arrive at such a conclusion was inexplicable. Of course, she didn't have schizophrenia. The idea was absurd.

When Tony had finished his line of reasoning, his eyes returned to his boss to find she was still watching him.

"I'm sorry," she said thoughtfully. "I know I'm not making any sense."

"Then explain it to me," Tony responded, willing himself to keep from disregarding her. He wanted anything but for Kristen to recede from speaking honestly with him.

"After my father passed away," Kristen began, "I started having dreams I attributed to the shock of losing him. They were intense dreams where I kept seeing this man I'd never met. And at the end of the dreams, I would wake up and find he was still with me. I saw him with my eyes just as I see you now."

Tony's eyebrows furrowed sharply at her words, and he had to force himself to relax.

"In the dreams," Kristen continued, "I didn't just see this man, but I began to see the experiences of other people with whom he'd come in contact. The most startling was of a woman named Pamela Hill. She lived here once—she sold my parents this house years ago. I never met her. I only learned her name a few weeks ago when I saw it on paperwork that listed her as a previous owner.

"I tracked Ms. Hill down at her retirement home, and she confided in me she's had the same dreams with this stranger. More to the point, he's the ghost of a man who died in this house."

Kristen's words incensed Tony. His eyes could see she was entirely sincere, though her words rang as a joke, a stupid prank his brothers might attempt to sell. Tony shook his head, holding her gaze.

"I know what you're thinking," she answered his unspoken response. "That I'm having you on."

"Aren't you?" Tony responded, allowing the smile he'd restrained to break on his face.

"Look at my eyes," she implored him. "Do you see a lie in them?"

Tony saw nothing in Kristen's eyes that gave her away, desperate as he was to find something to betray the woman's story.

"I don't believe in ghosts," he said, exhaling at a loss to say anything less uncomfortable.

"*You* don't? Tony, I'm a doctor of psychology. You're speaking to someone who works in a scientific field established specifically to disprove the existence of ghosts and spirits and demons and gods. I don't even believe we have souls—from my point of view, that's all a bunch of childish nonsense. And yet here I am, talking to someone I hardly know, admitting to something I would sooner shoot myself to avoid telling one of my friends or colleagues back home."

Tony felt the sting of her statement but didn't let his eyes leave her.

"If all that's true, then why are you allowing yourself to believe in it?" he asked bluntly. "Why are ghosts the answer to your experience, when you already know they aren't on the list of things that might explain it? I'm not saying I can explain why some lady is having the same dreams as you. But why would failing to see the right answer then open the door to one you *know* is untrue?"

Tony saw Kristen's eye twitch in response to his question, and she brought her hands to cover her face.

"Exactly," she said.

The front doorbell rang, inciting an immediate bark from Penelope that broke Tony's focus on Kristen. On the porch were three men who had quietly come from a large, faceless white van parked on the driveway.

Kristen pulled Penelope by her collar and walked her back to her bedroom to let Tony open the door and greet their visitors in peace.

"Good morning," one man responded to Tony's greeting. "We're here for Kristen Cole to perform a biohazard removal."

Tony extended his hand to each of them and welcomed the men inside, along with the large black cases of equipment they carried. As he led the men upstairs and into the master bedroom, all Tony could think of was what Kristen had said. He wasn't prepared to call the woman crazy, but it was clear she wasn't well.

CHAPTER TWENTY

K risten could barely believe she had taken Tony into her confidence about Valon. She must be desperate for support, the psychologist concluded. Again, Kristen's attempt to maintain a professional relationship with Tony resulted in an intimate blunder. At least his response had been kind. It would surprise Kristen if Tony nodded just to go about pretending she had never said a word to him.

But the dream of her mother still held strong in Kristen's mind. She considered dialing up her parent's friends but instantly rejected the notion. Kristen's mother would never have divulged such a secret to a girlfriend. She presumed Margaret Cole wasn't even close enough with her father to speak of such a matter.

Kristen's mother had maintained a diary of her cancer treatments, and the psychologist wondered now if the dying woman had noted any strange experiences she faced during chemotherapy. When Kristen arrived here days after her father's death, she had come across several notebooks stored in a box of her mother's possessions.

Just the sight of her mother's handwriting, making the

inanimate objects perfectly alive her mind, had proved too significant a challenge for Kristen. She refused to read them. There are levels of intimacy between a parent and child, and this was one Kristen would never feel comfortable perusing, even if the woman's death no longer made it a violation. But the need for Kristen to know she wasn't crazy ruled against her sense of propriety, and she eyed the cardboard boxes in the guest room corner, knowing she must try.

Kristen rose from the air mattress, attempting not to disturb Penny, who had just laid down beside her. She went directly for the first of two boxes marked 'Margaret,' handwritten by her father with a fat black Sharpie. Atop the brown cardboard sat the Ouija board game Kristen had chucked into the trash days ago. She thought Tony must've found it and set it in this room for her. Having no more patience for embarrassment, Kristen set it aside and pulled out the prize she was after.

From the first box, Kristen lifted out the three spiral notebooks, unexpectedly recognizing the belongings they sat among still carried her mother's scent. It was a dose of inescapable truth that reminded Kristen these were not merely relics of the past, but her mother's intimate possessions.

Penelope couldn't resist the opportunity to rise from bed and stick her nose in the box, which Kristen didn't bother to prevent. The woman returned to the mattress with her mother's notebooks, reached in her bag for a pen, and opened the first cover as if she were about to begin thorough scientific research.

Kristen surmised these journals were mostly notations of her mother's radiation and chemotherapy treatments. There were notations of how she'd felt from day to day, but Margaret included only the most straightforward descriptions; meals she skipped, how poorly she slept on certain days, or why she didn't go for a walk. Now and then, she included a smattering of extra insight, but she devoted these notes to her feelings about the treatments themselves or a critique of the doctor's input.

To Kristen's frustration, she found that the second notebook began with a dozen pages of the same benign information. Still, she forced herself to turn the pages one by one, resisting the desire to flip through them like a deck of cards.

And then, Kristen found an entry that stopped the growing anxiety in her hands. She landed upon several pages where each line on the paper was full of her mother's elegantly scripted handwriting.

May 24, 2015

Dick was sweet enough to move downstairs into the guest room last week. I explained how sleeping by a schedule has become impossible for me. The exhaustion of this disease makes little sense. Even if I sleep through the night, I still fight to keep my eyes from closing several times during the day. I've become an old cat in search of a new place to nap every few hours. I only wish I had a feline's strength during those waking hours. Still, I am no longer concerned about Dick's heavy feet waking me—he keeps to himself downstairs unless I call for him.

Dick's absence in my bed has also encouraged my friend. He visited me three times this week and showed me something new each time. I haven't bothered to discuss the dreams with Dr. Russell. I was told from the beginning of my treatment that wild dreams would happen. The poison stimulates the dream centers of the brain. I only mention them here because he insists that writing my dreams down will help me with interpreting and making sense of them. Evidently, we can learn much from our dreams, but our woken mind rarely has access to them. With this terrible cocktail, however, the dreams often seem more real than the waking world, and it's difficult to separate them.

For example, my sweet friend from UCLA. I have had more than a few dreams about him, who is someone I haven't seen for forty years. My first college sweetheart of all people. The dreams are indescribably vivid, not to mention racy. This morning I again woke to feel as if Chris Jackson was still twenty-one and courting me. I wake up giggling over how real the dreams seem. I don't even know if Chris Jackson is still alive. I might share my dreams with Dick if recounting past lovers to one's husband weren't the worst idea a wife could have. Dick and I haven't been sexual for at least ten years, but I can still picture the agitation on his face that time I mentioned Chris—when my husband and I were fighting just after Kristen was born.

Still, I'd like to share them with someone. It's just that I find them hysterical! I don't know how well it would go over with my Golden Girls Spades Club. I wish now I had joined a book club instead; some group of ladies enjoying *Fifty Shades of Grey*. They would surely appreciate hearing about the stuff Chris made me do when I was a girl.

Kristen started at her mother's words, written in black ink with penmanship she had never come close to achieving as a girl. She wanted nothing more than to find the pages of these diaries filled with anecdotes about the weather or who was causing trouble on *Days of Our Lives*. But Chris Jackson's name was there on the page, a name her mother never once mentioned to Kristen. Margaret once discussed how she had slept with a few young men before marriage. It was a vague example she offered Kristen during "the talk" when the girl reached twelve years old. But the discussion never included names or places, other than a simple, "…when I was at college." They didn't include building or classroom names, and Mom never mentioned the Roosevelt Hotel as the place where she lost her virginity.

She felt confounded by the relaxed manner Margaret wrote about her relationship with these men, particularly how she related them to Kristen's father. Yes, this was the woman's private journal, filled with accounts of a journey not meant for her daughter's eyes, but the woman's irreverence for Richard Cole stung and filled Kristen with nothing less than anger.

She'd never been close to her mother, not in the way she had been with her father. The man had been her world, the template against which she compared all men. The tone of her mother's disregard, even when Richard was all the woman had, ate at Kristen's composure, regardless of the discovery in her hands. Losing all patience, she leafed through the remaining pages of the second diary until she came to an entry that made her swear aloud.

August 4, 2015

The treatments have become more painful, just as the dreams have become more vivid. Last night, Chris came to me again, but he no longer looks like Chris. His eyes are not mischievous. Instead, they are dark and brooding. Even more disturbing, they are blue. Before I woke, he told me his name was not Chris. Instead, he called himself a name I've never heard before—I had to research it on the internet to conclude it is a real name—Valon. I don't know what to make of the change.

Kristen could never doubt herself again. The duties of scientific investigation were meaningless here. She held irrefutable proof in her very hands. If Kristen suffered from some version of schizophrenia, her variety would include vast periods of time-loss. During those periods, she would need to have been exposed to these diaries. But even if there weren't a dozen ways to refute that hypothesis, nothing could invalidate her conversation with Pamela Hill.

The ghost was real; these women's experiences and Kristen's own were real. Free of doubt, she aimed her every thought toward discovering all she could learn. She flipped through the remaining pages of the second notebook, finding nothing more, then reached for the third spiral, which was empty but for the first few pages. Her mother's handwriting here was sloppy as if she no longer could produce the letters as beautifully as she always had.

June 11, 2016

The pain will not subside now without Demerol, and the price of sleep is that I can't keep my mind focused when my eyes are open. Writing this—constructing sentences—remains the only way I can keep my mind from drifting. But it is so difficult to do. The nurse was frank that I don't have long. Then again, the doctor told me the same thing a year ago, and here I still am. Valon is my only real comfort. He takes me away every time I close my eyes, even if my body now cannot pair with him.

I begged Valon to let me stay here, to remain with him, but he insists I cannot. He says I will not see him again after I die. He won't tell me why our two spirits cannot be together. At first, I was angry with him for it, but now I don't think he understands the reason himself. Or perhaps he can't tell me.

I've never felt so loved in my life. The memories of Chris pale next to Valon's love. He makes me laugh and holds me close—the only two things I ever wanted in this life. Knowing it must end is more painful than this cancer. Valon tries to hide his fear from me, but I can tell he feels the same.

CHAPTER TWENTY-ONE

Kristen overcame her eagerness to show the diaries to Tony. Though it was a relief to confess her troubles, it was unfair to compel him to take on the role of her confessor. Tony was here to do a job, not hold her hand, and Kristen wouldn't allow herself to violate that working relationship any more than she had.

Still, resolving her doubt had changed everything for Kristen, and the clarity enabled her to think well for the first time in weeks.

"They're still upstairs?" Tony asked as she and Penelope arrived in the backyard. He moved the small plastic bowl holding his lunch away from the dog's mouth.

"They are," she confirmed. Kristen noticed the strange-looking meal in Tony's hands and nodded at it with a pained squint. "Do I need to order us some lunch?"

"What do you mean? It's wonderful," he chewed with mock confusion.

"It looks a little undercooked. Is it seasoned?"

"No, it's grilled plain," Tony answered. "There's seasoning in the quinoa."

"That's wonderful?" she asked suspiciously.

Tony smiled and took a sip from his green soda can.

"Gotta eat clean to stay lean," he said, "and it tastes just fine."

"You're staying lean drinking high fructose?" she raised an eyebrow.

"Nope, this is water," he answered.

"They serve water in soda pop cans now?"

"Well, its water with bubbles and a twist of lime. But, yes, they sell water in soda pop cans now."

"Oh, I see. How fancy. I suppose that's how all of this happens?" Kristen asked with a sly smile, waving her hand humorously at the young man's clothed physique.

"A lot of it, actually," he smiled back, lifting the can to toast her. "So, you're feeling better?"

"I'm doing much better," she acknowledged, realizing how humor had returned to her voice. "I'm grateful you let me talk to you earlier. It's helped organize my thoughts, and I'm ready to resolve my problems."

"Very good," Tony declared. "It helps to talk things through. I heard that from a shrink on the Oprah show when I was a kid."

Kristen couldn't help but laugh at the guy. She was grateful to have the man's level head around. Then Kristen jumped when Penelope released a succession of painfully loud barks before Tony could quiet her.

"Someone rang the doorbell," he confirmed when he'd quieted the dog, then rose to run out to attend to his next arrival of the day.

After leashing Penelope to the extended collar and filling her bowl with fresh water, Kristen followed in Tony's footsteps, happening upon him and a man who wore a Terminix uniform.

"Kristen, this is the exterminator, George," Tony said, interrupting himself to introduce her.

"It's good to meet you, George," Kristen answered, privately delighted that he hadn't shown up six hours later as the company threatened.

"Good to meet you, ma'am," the lanky blond responded.

"I mentioned our experience with Penelope scratching at the coat closet," Tony said to Kristen. "Do you want to tell him about your experience the other night?"

"Yes, please," she confirmed at his reminder. "My dog —she's the one you probably heard when you rang the bell—she woke me up in the middle of the night by growling at the wall. At first, I thought there was a bug or spider in the room, but I turned on the lights and couldn't find anything. After Penelope continued to growl at the wall, I thought of what Tony said right before he called you."

"You probably have a rodent infestation," George nodded. "I doubt your dog would wake you up over a bug —she'd probably just eat 'em."

"I placed traps in the closet," Tony said, pointing to the door that opened into the area under the stairway. "None of them have gone off, and I didn't see any droppings."

"Where were you when your dog woke you up?" George asked Kristen.

"In the guest room, back around there, off the hallway in the back. Would you like me to show you?" she offered.

"No, that's okay," he shook his head. "I just want to make sure you're not also finding them upstairs. If they're only in the walls down here, they're probably coming in from under the house. Have you checked the crawl space?"

"I haven't, but I can show you where it is," confirmed Tony.

"Great, let me start there," said George.

Tony led the exterminator outside toward the rear of the house where the crawlspace entrance lay.

From upstairs, Kristen heard footsteps descending and looked to find the cleanup crew, who carried down black bags and cases with their equipment. They each dressed in bulky grey plastic suits.

"Are you Miz Cole?" asked the third man in a near whisper. "We're all finished upstairs with the removal."

"I am," Kristen answered, mirroring his volume. "Is there anything you need? Shall I write you a check?"

"Oh, no, that's okay. Our office will send you a bill. I just need you to sign off on the work. Do you want to inspect the room?"

Kristen hesitated, looking out the southern windows for any sign of Tony.

"Could you wait a moment for me?" she asked, turning to the front door to go find the young man.

At the threshold, Kristen paused and turned back.

"Okay, I'll do it," she said, overcoming her reluctance in the face of embarrassment. "Will you come with me?"

"Sure thing," the man answered and extended his hand out for her to take the lead up the stairs.

Kristen's feet didn't spring forward as she wanted them to, but she moved nevertheless. When they finally arrived at the master bedroom door, her blood pressure had risen just enough from the climb that she couldn't be sure if the change were from terror or falling out of shape.

Kristen first noticed how the headboard no longer bore any of the black powder smudges left behind by the forensics team. They had pulled the bedsheets off the mattress and folded them, placing the linen on a corner armchair along with the two pillows. Turning to the bathroom, Kristen saw through the opened door that the floor was clean of the dried bloodstains. There was a heavy smell of lemon cleaner in place of the dried urine she'd caught yesterday. However, under that lemon was a harsh scent with which she was unfamiliar. Kristen inhaled sharply to clear her sinuses.

"You can probably smell the agent we used to remove the infections material," the cleaner said. "We use a regular cleaner once we're done to mitigate the smell. We've left the window open to help the floor dry, but it will be a couple more days before the smell goes away. It's like when you paint a house—the fumes take a while to clear."

"That's fine," responded Kristen, staring at the bathroom floor from the threshold. "What do you need me to sign?"

He extended a clipboard holding the release document, its blank signature line circled. When Kristen had provided her autograph to the cleaner, both left and returned downstairs.

"Thank you very much for your assistance," she offered somberly at the front door.

"You're welcome. Good day to you," the quiet man replied plainly before exiting.

Kristen returned upstairs, bent on placing herself back in the master bedroom. Though she felt sure of herself, the psychologist didn't want to avoid the room. Fear was a funny thing—it could return at any moment if you avoided it.

Empty and quiet, Kristen found it was just a room. She entered and sat down on the uncovered mattress, hearing the slight creak of the heavy wooden bed frame underneath. From over her shoulder, Kristen glanced toward the bathroom, its door still wide open. She remembered the night Ryan had gone in there, and before the fear and panic of the next morning could follow the memory, Kristen stood again and went to it.

It was a technique called flooding. If you had an intense fear, called a phobia, the best way to overcome it was to flood the senses. If snakes horrified a patient, Kristen would arrange for them to visit the home of a pet owner. The process would start by its owner holding the snake from across the largest room in the house. Because a phobia is an irrational fear, the patient would immediately panic, even if the serpent were so far away they couldn't be of danger.

A natural limitation of panic is that humans can only maintain its assault on the body for a solid five minutes before the brain cuts off those taxing reactions. It's too much for the circulatory system to take any longer, so the brain shuts off the response to preserve the body's well-being. And so, every five minutes, the snake owner would be instructed to move a few feet closer to the patient.

While the patient would experience the alarming panic again, it would subside like clockwork when the body couldn't bear it any longer. After adjusting to the serpent's presence via this method, a patient would find they were no longer irrationally afraid of it. Kristen would usually allow the patient to end the therapy at a five-foot distance. After all, a healthy respect for snakes is not a disorder. But more often, the patient would ask to touch the snake or even request to hold it.

With that goal set in mind, Kristen walked to the bathroom door threshold and waited until the fear subsided. Then, she took two steps inside, standing on the nearly dried tile floor. While Kristen's breath increased in the face of her overwhelming situation, the woman stood her ground and waited for the fear to subside. When it finally did, Kristen took another two steps forward.

Standing now at the first of the double sinks, she looked up into the wall-sized mirror. Kristen could see most of the room around her. At last, when she'd taken the whole thing in, Kristen looked up at her face. There were tears in her eyes, but she blinked and pushed them away.

Kristen had done it—she was no longer a hostage to her fear.

Looking in the mirror, she remembered Pamela Hill as she had stood there in the 1990s. That day when the woman opened the medicine cabinet to pull out a bottle of painkillers. The woman had poured the bottle's entire contents into her hand, contemplating suicide, only to change her mind and settle for one pill to calm her pain.

She thought of the woman's words, how she'd said that Kristen needed to get out of the house. She saw the fear in the woman's eyes. But Kristen had just proven to herself that she wouldn't be controlled by fear, no matter how terrified Hill's words had made her.

Kristen watched her face and whispered a single word to the glass.

"Valon?"

From her periphery, Kristen saw a dark figure appear at the door frame to her right.

CHAPTER TWENTY-TWO

The Terminix exterminator inched his way out from under the house and was back onto the concrete pavement of the rear driveway when Tony heard car doors slamming.

"Well, I can't find anything," George said with impatience as he wiped at the dirt on his jumpsuit. "No droppings at all, and I didn't see any holes into the subflooring. So they must be getting in from somewhere on the perimeter. I'll do a spot check."

The words didn't register with Tony as he looked to see the clean-up crew's white van roll back down the driveway from behind his work truck.

"Okay, sir?" George asked.

"Sorry," Tony's attention jerked back before he replayed the man's words in his mind. "Yeah, that's fine."

"Do you want to take care of your dog for me, please?" he asked, again leading Tony's absent mind.

"Tell you what, check on the front of the house first, would you?" Tony asked. "I need to go check on Ms. Cole for a minute. Cool?"

"That's fine," replied George with a hint of confusion, and he began to pace the perimeter of the house.

Tony hurried back inside, finding his way to the rear hallway. Arriving at the guest room, he discovered its door wide open and the room empty. Tony called out Kristen's name, but no answer came. When he realized she must be upstairs, he moved gingerly, apprehensive of finding the poor woman in a similar emotional place as the day before.

Tony climbed the stairs and moved through the upper hall to the master bedroom, where he found the door wide open. The clean-up crew had left a strong odor behind them, something harshly tangy mixed with a wave of Lemon Pledge. *Shitrus*, he thought, seeing the bedroom windows open, no doubt left that way by the cleaners to air the space out.

As he inhaled to call out to find her, Tony turned his head and saw Kristen standing in the master bathroom at the double-sink counter. She stared at herself silently in the mirror. The floor was slightly wet, and she had left a few footprints, but it was undoubtedly clean—the crew had done their job.

Tony heard Kristen whisper something to him, but he couldn't make out the word as he moved to the doorframe.

"You okay?" asked Tony.

Kristen's head jerked toward him. She gasped lightly, bringing her hand to her mouth to cover it.

In his bid to be quietly respectful, Tony had startled the poor girl, and he was immediately regretful when he saw her process it with frustration. Tears were filling Kristen's eyes, and she failed to control them as a pained expression seized her face.

Tony stepped forward and tenderly placed his arms around Kristen and sighed at his blunder.

"I'm so sorry," he whispered in her ear.

"No, it wasn't you," she protested with a shake of her head. "I did that to myself."

Kristen smiled and wiped at her eyes, pulling back to look up into Tony's eyes.

"I wanted to come up here and face my fear," she continued, "and I did it. I will be just fine, I promise."

"That's good to hear," said Tony, relieved that Kristen's spirits remained optimistic, that his clumsiness hadn't upset her further.

She placed her arms around the young man's torso to hug him. Falling back into his chest, Kristen also allowed Tony to return his arms around her slight frame. Thoughts of keeping his distance left his mind—she didn't seem to want this hug to end quickly. She held on to the young man indefinitely, laying her head firmly at the crook of his neck.

Tony fought his inclination to release Kristen when her arms didn't relax their grip. Instead, he moved his hands slowly along her upper back, allowing himself to feel the warmth of the woman's body. Tony desperately wanted her, wanted this feeling.

As he moved, Tony felt Kristen's lungs breath against him, moving just enough to stimulate him. He felt his cock stiffen and couldn't help but allow himself to pull Kristen's body firmly against his.

Tony raised a gentle hand to cradle the back of her head, then turned his face and kissed her cheek. To his surprise, Kristen turned to meet his kiss with her lips, gently at first, and soon with a desire to match his own.

From behind him, Tony heard the bathroom door slam with a ferocious crack, causing his chest and shoulders to contract. The enormous pressure of the sound brought a scream from Kristen, who pulled violently from him.

"The wind," he said, allowing himself to release a bit of laughter once he understood what just happened. "The windows in the bedroom are open like this one. Got us a cross breeze going on here."

When her breathing slowed, Kristen pulled back further from him with awkwardness.

"I'm sorry," she said, looking down.

"No, don't worry about it," Tony smiled, not wanting to provide her with any excuse to feel regretful about what they'd just done. "Come on, I need to help the exterminator, and you can keep Penny from trying to play with him."

Tony turned and opened the door, then took a heavy pillar candle from atop the counter and placed it against the door's base.

"There, that ought to keep it open as the breeze airs the room out," Tony said, and he stood at the side to open the pathway for Kristen to pass. He maintained his smile, acting as if he were perfectly happy, though he could see the interruption of their intimacy had adversely affected Kristen.

But in moments, Kristen's face relaxed, and she walked forward as if nothing had happened. Tony followed her footsteps, and they left the master suite in silence.

Arriving on the first floor, they saw George standing on the front porch, tapping into his cellphone.

"Hi, are you ready?" the exterminator asked Tony when he emerged through the front door.

"Sure," he replied. "Kristen will help with the dog for us. I take it you found nothing in the front?"

"No, there's nothing," George shook his head. "I found something I'll show you when we're done. You don't have termites, but there's a section on the north end of your home you'll want to have me spray to ensure they don't settle there."

"Damn it," Tony sighed.

"No, it's fine. It's just simple maintenance, I promise, but you don't want to ignore it," he assured the anxious young man.

"We're renovating to sell the house," Kristen chimed in, "so won't we need to tent the house before we sell anyhow?"

"Yeah, any inspector or buyer will ask you to do that for a structure this old," George confirmed.

"It will be fine," said Tony, struggling to keep his attitude light.

When they arrived at the gate to the rear yard, Tony entered first to an excitable Penelope, who already smelled the visitor. As a rule, the Husky was kept separated from any workmen on the property. Her fluffy curl of a tail wiggled emphatically now at the prospect of finally being introduced to one of them.

"Penny, sit," said Tony firmly, and the dog's back end touched the ground without a moment's indecision.

Her eyes sparkled as Tony kneeled beside the animal and took hold of her collar. Penny sneaked in two quick licks on his cheek, unable to control herself.

"Do you mind meeting her before you begin back here?" he asked George. "It will help her calm down."

"Hello," the exterminator said with a slight nod of his head to Penny as if he were at a cocktail mixer at the United Nations, and Tony was his interpreter.

"Put your hand out like this so she can sniff you," Tony said with a smirk and placed his hand forward with a loose fist to show the man.

George mimicked the move and lowered his hand

down to Penny's level with only a little hesitation. Within two seconds, the dog had sniffed her new acquaintance's skin and offered a full lick of welcome to her backyard. The gesture evoked a grin from the exterminator, and he ventured to open his palm to rub the side of Penny's face, sending her into a rumble of joyful wagging.

"She's a sweet girl," George commented, which sent the Husky further into ecstasy.

"Kristen, would you hold her, please?" Tony asked, and the woman moved to take his place beside her dog.

George remained fixed on his new friend until Tony's voice snapped him back to attention.

"You're good to go," the young man gestured with his head toward the house.

"Okay," the exterminator confirmed and resumed his duty.

He pushed aside plants and bushes to get a clear line of sight for every inch of the rear perimeter, stopping now and then to touch wood where he remarked his concern for its solidity.

"It only takes a hole the size of a quarter," he told Tony. "Once they manage that, there will be a colony within weeks."

George's methodical examination lasted ten minutes before he stopped and stood with dismay, his brow furrowed sharply. He lifted his hand to shield his eyes from the mid-day sun and looked up at the second floor.

"They must be coming in from the top," George declared, scanning all around to see what trees were close enough to the house that rodents could use them to enter from the roof. The nearest pine branch was over twenty feet from the structure.

"Only Mighty Mouse could leap that far," George said

absently. "The only remaining option would be the electrical cables attached to the house from the street."

Both men returned through the north side entrance to the front of the house. Tony saw what the exterminator already realized. The electrical wires from the pole on the street shot down into the ground at the curb. The city delivered the house power underground through pipes that must run up the lot's slope beside the driveway. Not a single wire touched the home's second floor.

———

Kristen didn't partake much in what little conversation Tony offered during their ride to the gym for that night's shower. If there were no rodents in the house, she felt confident Valon's presence had agitated Penelope. Having woken from another shared dream, Kristen presumed the ghost was nearby, and her dog must've sensed him.

"The exterminator might be right. The noise bothering Penny might be something else entirely," Tony suggested on their ride back to Kristen's house. "Temperature changes in the plumbing could cause that noise. Maybe the water heater is arbitrarily seeping into the system even when the taps are closed. I'll talk to our new guy about it when he comes by tomorrow."

"I'm sure it's something simple like that," she responded without conviction.

Kristen had avoided all mention of their kiss. The slamming of the bathroom door had shaken her, and she was confident Valon had been in the room with them. At first, she hesitated at receiving Tony's advances, but Kristen then gave into them when she found she needed his touch.

Her motivation was more than just his sweet kisses. Part of Kristen wanted to know—she wanted one more bit of proof that the ghost was with her. Kristen had called Valon's name aloud, and when Tony appeared instead of the spirit, she allowed the young man to have his way with her. It was a mindless and childish taunt, but the ferocity of the slam cured Kristen of any petulance left in her.

The true challenge facing the woman now was that her selfish lapse had inadvertently forced her to recognize her intense attraction to Tony. Feeling his hands hold her was another reminder of the strength of his presence. It was no small feat to stop herself from inviting the young man inside as he pulled the truck up to the curb in front of her house.

"I'll see you tomorrow," Tony said without catching Kristen's long peer at his handsome face.

He was so ridiculously beautiful. But this felt like more than simple lust—Kristen needed him, the smell and taste of him. Her eyes wandered over his arms and hands as they gripped the steering wheel. To have them touch her again, even if only for just a little while. Kristen considered suggesting Tony should take her to his workshop and van. Would that ensure his safety from Valon? Would being away from the house stop the ghost as it had for Pamela Hill, or would Valon's anger wait for them to return in the morning?

After a thought of Penelope, Kristen reached to gather her bag and pulled on the door handle to let herself out.

"Thanks, Tony," said Kristen gratefully. "I'll see you tomorrow."

CHAPTER TWENTY-THREE

Valon loved Margaret. There was no doubt in his mind.

He had loved Pamela as well, but their connection had been so different. Valon's red-haired lover of over twelve years hadn't been less intimate with him than Margaret was now. Even when settling for the form of another man, the veneer of Pamela's dead husband, Valon had felt every morsel of their passion, allowing the woman to share herself with him.

The difference was that Pamela didn't love Valon; she loved Bobby Hill. And even when the ghost adopted the woman's fantasies, speaking in the man's voice, answering questions just as her husband would, Pamela could only love his memory. When Valon tried to explain, to show he was someone else, the woman rejected him almost completely. Yes, she would allow him to pleasure her, but she rejected the young stranger with steel-blue eyes by denying him her heart. And Pamela had walked away from Valon. She left the ghost's presence as if he was something unholy—an addiction from which she must sever all ties, or they would consume her.

It had almost destroyed him, the pain of her rejection, and the absence of her voice in the house.

When he found Margaret asleep in his bed that first night, he probed her mind in search of a new disguise, eager to find the lover of her dreams, desperate to regain the affection he'd been without. The ghost had led Margaret to her memories without the slightest effort. It was as if they were restlessly waiting to comfort them both—the tall and masculine Chris Jackson, with his devilish good looks and charm. Adopting his guise had been a pleasure for the ghost if only to experience the wild desire which Margaret looked upon the boy.

And then, when Valon had finally sated his pressing needs, he changed his mind. He allowed the woman to see his true image. Unlike with Pamela Hill, the ghost found only puzzlement and excitement in Margaret's eyes at the sight of him. She didn't quite believe what she saw at first, sure the potent cocktail of poison prescribed by her doctors was altering her wild visions. But in time, the woman did not care if Valon was real. Margaret was grateful to have him take her away from the pain within her body.

And then something happened that changed everything for Valon: Margaret loved him. He had felt it in her words, in her touch, in her eyes, and with every breath. She delighted at his caress, and he laughed for hours at her wicked sense of humor. Margaret could see him when she was awake. Regardless of how much energy it took the ghost to gather himself to material form, he gladly exhausted himself to see Maggie's eyes shine when she noticed him. It was like living an eternity in nine short months. And Valon held tight to the sharp light of that joy when the dying woman's words became agonizingly painful for her to vocalize.

"Richard is going to have them transfer me to the hospice," she said, her eyes all but closed.

"He mustn't," said Valon, his strong face immediately agitated. "I won't let him take you away from me."

The ghost had known this day was coming. Margaret had accepted her death and explained what would happen several times over the past weeks. There was nothing to be done. All Margaret could do was wait for the insidious cancer to finish destroying every system in her body. And when the Demerol was no longer capable of easing the pain enough for her to sleep, they would take her to a hospice to wait as the final hours and minutes of her life passed.

"Stop it, my love, please. I must go. My time is up, can't you see?" she asked weakly through labored breaths. "You told me I couldn't remain here with you when I die. So, what difference will a few hours make?"

Valon touched her face with his hand and caressed her, running his fingers over her lips. He had never felt such pain in his life.

"Please, don't do that, my love. Everything," she said, closing her eyes in agony, "everything hurts."

When Margaret's eyes finally opened again, Valon brought every sub-atomic bit of material in his ethereal form together to lie beside her on the bed. He was adamant that she would see him. Valon would have her feel his breath, warm and alive, as it flowed painlessly over her body.

"I need you to take care of Richard for me," Margaret finally said.

Valon scowled in confusion as much as in protest.

"No, you must do this for me," she stopped him before he could speak. "Richard is a good man. He has been a far better husband to me than I deserved—far better than I ever was a wife to him. He's been here every day taking care of me. I was selfish to have him buy this house. We didn't need all this, and now his retirement is ruined on account of it. He'll have to sell the house or go back to work. Either way, I want you to make sure he's safe. I want him to find someone who will love him, who will bring him the happiness he deserves."

"I don't want him in this house when you are gone," said Valon with a heavy voice, almost desperate to resist her pained request. "What could I possibly do to help him?"

"Help to ease his mind," she answered. "You know how to do that. When he's asleep—make his dreams peaceful. He'll recover in time; I know he will."

Valon shook his head, unwilling to even consider it.

"Promise me," Margaret said, her voice becoming locked in her throat as a spasm fought to capture the words. "Promise me."

Valon exhaled, defeated to give her any other answer.

"I promise," he said, reaching to touch her hand as lightly as he could.

The words seem to release weight from the dying woman's chest, and she could breathe better in the silence that followed.

"Thank you, my love," Maggie said, her last spoken words to him.

The attendants of the hospice center arrived that afternoon and transferred Margaret's small, ravaged frame onto a gurney. Soon enough, they carried her down the stairs and out to their vehicle. Valon could not see through the open door but watched through the windows as the heavy truck doors closed the woman inside. He would never see Margaret with his eyes again.

The rest of the day went quickly, followed by the

evening that surrendered gracefully to the dark of night. Richard returned to the house, but Valon could tell in the man's eyes that Maggie still held on to her life. The grief had seemed to make him exhausted, and the older man went to bed. That Richard could do such a thing as sleep irritated Valon almost to anger, but he allowed the man to slumber in silence—the only sound left in the house.

Just after three o'clock in the morning, Richard's cell phone rang. A volunteer at the hospice announced herself and told Richard the time was near.

"I'm coming now," Cole said, and he moved as quickly as he could while sleep fell away from his mind, allowing him to balance his legs.

The man was gone for less than an hour before he returned through the front door, drawing Valon's attention and quick approach. Cole's eyes said it all—their weariness and defeat. Margaret was dead.

Anger.

A fury threatened to explode from Valon. He wanted to rip every door off its hinges, toss every stick of furniture at the man until he was dead. Valon would tear at his flesh until there was nothing left of Richard to burden him any longer.

But then the ghost saw Cole fall into the armchair by the living room fireplace and begin to weep. The man's hands trembled as heavy sobs came from his chest, threatening to stop him from breathing. He was devastated, this man who Maggie didn't even love, and he was alone.

At once, the fury fell away from Valon, disappearing like everything always did from him. He sat down on the sofa beside Richard and wept alongside the man for his love that was no more.

CHAPTER TWENTY-FOUR

Kristen awoke from the dream because Penelope sniffed and licked her earlobe. The woman would never be a morning person, and Penelope's kisses were a far more satisfying way to awaken than a screeching alarm clock. Also, the Husky had ensured Kristen's sleep schedule was both consistent and reliable; two factors that ensured she was more rested in the morning.

Kristen had never woken to find Valon lying beside her when Penelope was at her side. While he remained in her dreams, the ghost avoided her dog. But unlike before, Kristen now remembered her dreams well after she woke, regardless if Valon purposely bridged them into consciousness. She remembered every moment of the ghost's last day with Margaret Cole.

Kristen was never close to her mother, at least never close enough to satisfy her. She maintained that opinion into adulthood, even though it would be a lie to say her mother was genuinely distant. Perhaps Kristen's perception of their lukewarm relationship was partly in thanks to the exceptional closeness she felt with her father. Richard

Cole had been Kristen's heart—the person she compared every living soul against. Their relationship resulted from pure love and acceptance of each other. Whenever Kristen spoke to her father, she could be her true self. The usual pretense found in most relationships had never really existed between father and daughter, certainly not since she had matured into a young woman. Richard Cole's character and immediacy had never afforded the possibility of it.

Observing her mother through Valon's eyes had changed everything for Kristen, revealing a different woman than she'd ever known. Margaret Cole was often vain, vapid, childish, and petty—characteristics that had driven Kristen to despise the woman when she was a girl. But, as with all people, those traits were hardly a representation of the whole woman. Richard Cole had once asked Kristen to look in the mirror as she berated her mother's behavior. His unvarnished truth had wounded the girl as strongly as it had forced insight and humility. But it had never revealed the truth of who Margaret Cole was. Through Valon's dream, Kristen observed grateful kindness, reverence, and love for her father, and she believed her mother's words had been sincere.

Only seconds after Penelope arrived at her favorite corner of the front lawn to relieve herself, Tony's truck pulled up into the driveway. His arrival offered the Husky a prime opportunity to race and greet him without leashes or walls to hinder her hasty joy.

"Good morning," Kristen called with words that were no match for Penelope's emphatic welcome.

"Good morning, ladies," Tony replied, offering the dog a thorough head rub before setting about the morning's business.

"Everything was good last night," added Kristen. "We

both slept well. There wasn't a peep out of her—no rats to speak of."

"I'm going to go into the living room closet after Kim arrives. Since Penelope has scratched most at the rear of the living room closet, I'll take off some of the paneling and cut into the wall. If I don't find sawdust and droppings there, I don't know what I'll do."

"Sounds good," Kristen concurred.

No sooner did Kristen answer than Andrew Kim's van pulled up into the driveway. Tony let out a small gesture of triumph to see the vehicle arrive. Kristen could sense it took all the young man's effort not to walk up to the middle-aged plumber and high-five him.

"Glad to see you're already here," said Andrew Kim when he finally emerged from his driver's seat. "It's a bit of a pet peeve of mine—when I show up for the first day, and the site manager is nowhere to be found."

"I'm glad to be here," Tony countered with a smile.

"We're gonna get along just fine," the man returned, "especially if your check clears."

"Excellent," Tony answered with an anxious laugh.

Kristen understood she was watching the beginning of a love affair. She walked Penelope around the house to attach the animal to the extended leash in the backyard before feeding and watering her. By the time Kristen returned, the two men were already setting up. Tony's joy, unmistakably plastered across his face, let her know she could start her day.

———

ANDREW KIM STARED INTENSELY at the blueprint in Tony's hands, then up at the dining room wall.

"Your initial assessment when you looked at the

exposed wall from the bathroom side was correct: the main pass to the second floor doesn't go straight up," said Tony, pointing to the water and drain lines. "For whatever reason, both pipes turn horizontally and enter from the opposite side of the upstairs bathroom. But, look here, they still snake back around on the second floor."

"I've seen that before," Kim responded. "If the initial build goes in stages, but the plans change along the way, builders will compensate by rerouting the piping, instead of opening a wall up. Redoing finished work is significantly more expensive. I would guess the upstairs bathroom was originally designed to have its outlets in a different configuration, but when they started upstairs, the plans changed."

Tony stared at Kim, bewildered by the idea of building a home in stages where the first floor finished before the second floor started.

"You see this oak paneling?" Kim continued, running his hand over the dining room wall. "If they finished installing it before they ever worked on the upstairs, it would be cheaper to send the pipes backward than ask their carpenter to remove all this molding, only to reinstall it. Of course, that decision was just asking for problems. If the zig-zag leaks, you're looking at a ten-fold bill to repair it. Since we need to replace it all, I'll send it straight up."

Tony studied the wall, seeing that Kim meant to open a section only three feet away from the closet. It might solve two problems at once, allowing him to remove the piping and expose the rat infestation in one cut.

"I can pull the paneling off while you set up," offered Tony. "It'll only take me a few minutes."

"Perfect," Kim conceded. "I'll unload my materials while you take care of that."

Tony nodded before the plumber turned and headed back out to his van. In moments, Kim brought several buckets-worth of gear inside, along with an adjustable steel ladder and bundles of heavy copper product, laying them all on the floor. Tony promptly removed the crown from the wall and pulled off the molding that exposed the three darkly stained panels. These he gently popped off, managing not to damage any of them. At last, Tony presented the uncovered sheetrock.

"If you want to use those sawhorses and boards to make a table for yourself, please be my guest," offered Tony as he drew Kim's attention to his woodwork setup in the far corner of the living room.

"Don't mind if I do," Kim gratefully accepted.

By the time the plumber had moved the setup and laid out his tools on the makeshift table, Tony had cut a large rectangular section of sheetrock by hand to expose the studs.

Just as the young man had deduced, the unusual and dangerous piping configuration was present.

"Oh yeah," said Kim, appraising the expected work, "and thankfully, I don't see any leaking."

Kim looked to Tony, expecting a response to his observation, but the young man studied the exposed wall, running his fingers over the studs and shining a light down to the interior wall base.

"Is everything okay?" Kim asked after receiving silence from the young man.

"I feared there might be rodents in the walls," Tony answered, his eyes fixed on the grooves of the timber and exposed spaces. "The dog has been randomly growling at the walls as if she can hear them scratching, but I see nothing here to show their presence."

"That's good news," said Kim.

"Very good news. That check's gonna clear now for sure," Tony smiled. "I expected that rats would blow the owner's budget out of the water."

Tony was immediately sorry for the joke, fearful he may have given the man a false impression of his reliability, but Kim released a hearty chuckle.

"If the dog hears things in the wall, it could very well be that," Kim pointed at the extraneous piping. "All those cuts increase the opportunity for cavitation when the water temperature changes. The dog might be hearing the metal expanding and contracting."

"Great," Tony shot back enthusiastically. "Hopefully, this will solve that."

"I want to double-check that the previous guy shut off the water before I begin. Where is the main?" Kim asked.

"By the water heater in the laundry room off the kitchen. Just over there," said Tony, taking a step into the kitchen to point to the door.

"Thanks, I'll be right back," said Kim, who stepped away.

Alone, Tony couldn't stop himself from releasing a silent interpretive dance of joy, the robust choreography based on his dad's favorite Michael Jackson moves, included an exuberant crotch grab in homage to the late pop singer. When Tony finished, he did a double-take to ensure he had been alone. The last thing he needed was for Kim to walk in on such a display.

"It's ready to go," Kim announced as he returned to the dining room.

"What can I do to assist you?" Tony asked.

"Oh, I'll be fine," the man shook off the offer. "I don't want to keep you from whatever else you've got going on."

"If you're sure," said Tony, privately hoping Kim would allow him to watch his work.

"I'm just going to be cutting out the old piping for the first hour," said Kim, "but I appreciate the offer. I'll let you know if I need anything."

"Wonderful, thank you," nodded Tony.

"Thank you," Kim man nodded back, setting his ladder next to the exposed wall as he prepared to start at the top.

Tony left Kim in possession of the room and walked to update Kristen about the noise. Arriving at the guest room, he found the door wide open.

"The plumber is about to make a lot of noise for the next hour or so," Tony said when Kristen raised her eyes in question. "You might want to slip on some headphones or move out back and enjoy the day."

"I was just getting ready to take Penelope on a run," she answered.

"Good idea," replied Tony, sporting a thumbs up at the woman.

A second later, Kim's hand saw released a terrible racket as the blade cut into the fifty-year-old galvanized pipes. It was to be a slow process, cutting into the metal, but it was still the quickest way to remove the old material and make way for the new.

Tony returned along the hallway path he'd come from, stopping in the kitchen to find his earplugs. Before he could slip the fluorescent nubs in, the young man heard a startling pop followed by a terrible crash that replaced the cutting metal grind.

"FUCK!" Kim screamed awkwardly through clenched teeth.

His handsaw fell in an uproar of clatter as it hit everything it could. The vibrating blade and gravity conspired to deliver the machine violently to the floor. Tony leaped forward to pull the cord from the wall, a feat he managed despite the powerful electric shock he received. Shaking off the painful jolt instinctively, Tony saw that Kim had somehow kept his balance atop the six-foot ladder.

With a quick thrust of movement, the feet of Kim's ladder swept out as if someone kicked them. The man grabbed ahold of the steel only to be pulled over by it, his head barely avoiding the edge of the makeshift table beside him as he crashed painfully to the floor on his side.

Tony moved as quickly as he could to reach Kim, placing his hands on the man while the plumber screamed in pain from the injury to his back and ribs. From the backyard, Penny released a volley of angry barks at the ominous sounds. Looking up, Tony saw Kristen standing in horror at the scene.

CHAPTER TWENTY-FIVE

"He'll be fine," Tony said to Kristen after he bid farewell to Kim and his two sons. The two older boys had visited the house to collect their father's belongings. "He blames himself entirely for the accident."

The fall had shaken Kristen—she couldn't understand why Valon would attack Kim. She bit her tongue as Tony's referred to the event as "the accident."

Kim's leather gloves had dampened the force of the electric shock, but the jolt was still powerful enough for the plumber to lose control of the tool. The noise of the saw falling from Kim's hands had brought Kristen running out of her room, but she had seen the poor man's fall with her own eyes. She would never forget witnessing the bottom of his ladder jerk out from underneath him as if by an invisible kick. The man fell and missed the end of the makeshift wooden stand by barely an inch, leaving no question in Kristen's mind as to Valon's role in the miserable event.

Kim may have escaped a head injury, but his back had not been so lucky. The plumber refused Kristen's notion to call an ambulance but allowed Tony to take him to the emergency room. After hours of waiting, they released Kim high as a kite with a bagful of prescription painkillers in hand and strict orders to remain in bed. The ER doctor promised that a week off his feet would allow Kim's bruised ribs and sprained back muscles to heal. The man's wife and sons came at once when he called them from the hospital. The boys helped to load their father's truck with his tools, and the elder son drove the van home.

"He promised to let me know when he can return," Tony went on. "He already had other jobs lined up for when he would finish here, so he may have to come back afterward."

"I'm sure he would understand if you needed to call in a replacement," Kristen suggested lightly.

"Indefinite flexibility is the unfortunate nature of this business. But another replacement?" the young man sighed heavily. "I think it's worth waiting a week before we pull that trigger."

"But, you'll still look around?" Kristen asked, careful to speak without a hint of aggression.

"Of course," Tony nodded.

"Are you okay?" she asked. "You said you weren't hurt before you left, but was that true?"

"I'm fine," Tony shook his head as if it were nothing. "I got a small zap when I pulled the cord out, but it was over in a second. I didn't even remember it after the poor guy fell."

"What do you think caused the ...accident?" she asked, looking down at the wall socket, now surrounded by dark streaks of scorching.

"I would guess the wiring for the house is out of code," Tony responded. "I doubt it's been a problem before. A space heater was likely the strongest pull on our wiring in the past. That electric handsaw Kim was using draws twice the amount of juice."

Kristen didn't respond.

"Any tool with a three-prong plug operates safely from a standard socket," he continued. "I'm guessing the cause was on our end. If it was drawing too much current, the system should have shut the circuit or plug off. Haven't you ever used a hairdryer that popped the power? I've come across several indications the builders cut corners in the construction of this house. The very pipes he was attempting to remove are an example of cost-savings winning out over function," Tony pointed to the exposed wall as if it were in the middle of open-heart surgery. "Then again, the shock might also mean his saw was defective."

Again, Kristen didn't respond to Tony's explanation. She had nothing else to say. Her mind remained consumed with a quiet resolve—she could not trust the ghost. But what could Kristen do if they weren't safe in the light of day? Would Valon let her ask him? If Tony had been on that ladder, Kristen would never have forgiven herself.

"Yeah, I'm not fucking thrilled about this either," he answered her expressionless face.

Kristen looked to Tony, pulled out of her thoughts, perplexed by his unexpected change.

"Well, you're just standing there, pouting like this was my fault," he declared. "I wasn't to know any of this would happen. It was an accident, not our destiny."

Kristen became aware of her stance, how she'd allowed herself to appear.

"I don't think this was your fault at all," Kristen said, approaching the young man calmly when she'd managed to compose herself. "I'm glad you were here. I mean it."

Tony's eyes softened at her conciliation, visibly relieved to hear Kristen's words.

"I'm frustrated is all. When I think—"

"I'm frustrated too," he answered over her, unable to relieve the defensive timbre of his voice entirely.

"I know," Kristen breathed.

Tony's eyes found Kristen after he'd walked around in a circle, obviously upset. In them, she saw more than she expected at the moment. He stared at her as if he'd been worked up for something more than a quiet apology.

Tony approached Kristen and took her hand to lead her into the other room. It was an intimate gesture that she didn't pull away from, but she wouldn't let him take her here—not now that she understood the danger.

"Not here," she whispered. "Take me to your shop—to your van."

Tony didn't pretend to hear Kristen and continued to lead her toward the guest room.

"Not here, Tony" she repeated herself, pulling her arm a bit in resistance.

"For what?" he turned with a dubious sigh.

"I won't be able to relax," she answered. "Not after what…"

Tony took hold of her and kissed, silencing her words and letting her feel his thirst. She didn't stop him, but her mind battled with the moment, searching for a way to stop him.

Just a few moments, Kristen told herself. If it happened quickly, nothing would harm them, as nothing had in the past. It was a stretch of logic filled with so many holes she didn't trust it for a second. But Tony pulled to draw her into his arms, taking control of her with his wet kisses, and she lost her line of reasoning to the deafening pleasure of the young man.

KRISTEN UNDERSTOOD the sun was low in the sky when she opened her eyes and saw the dim glow of daylight outside the window.

Tony lay beside her, his eyes closed and fast asleep. The boy's passion had been ravenous, and he had taken much more from Kristen than their previous couplings had. Tony needed more from her than just sex; the tenderness of his urgency made his needs clear—he wanted her to desire him.

Even in her exhausted state, Kristen knew the danger she'd placed him in, just by having him there. She needed Tony to leave at once. Tonight, Kristen would reason with Valon, or she would destroy him.

"Will you take me to shower up at the gym, please?" she asked, gently patting Tony's chest as she laid her head upon it.

"Mm-hmm," Tony agreed quietly without opening his eyes or mouth.

Kristen's eyes closed as she breathed in the sweet musk of his skin, the heaviness of sleep taking over again.

Just five more minutes, she thought.

CHAPTER TWENTY-SIX

At the back of the living room closet, Valon slid
aside the panel masking his father's secret
hiding place. He gently placed the wooden box
into the small dark space between him and the bathroom,
which even the most thorough burglar or police officer
would never find.

Valon couldn't help but open the box to look upon the
artifact one more time before shutting it away. Pulling the
packing fabric back, he could see the crown glinting even
in the dim light available at the back of the closet. Valon
ran his fingers along the exquisite circle with its carvings
of bird feathers set around the perimeter. They looked like
ocean waves of gold that radiated back from the forehead
where two bird talons held a large red jewel. Valon
touched it with his thumb, and at once, the man's sight
left him.

In the darkness, he saw colors in his mind, and a
vision of a dim chamber lit by torches. On the floor before
him kneeled people who wore masks covered in raven
feathers. They held out their hands to Valon as if in praise
—as if they prayed to him.

Valon's released the crown with a jolt of panic, and his vision returned. The man moved like a stunned animal backward and out of the closet. Fear pushed his limbs before he could collect his wits, and somehow he headed toward the front door to flee.

Before Valon's hand could grasp the handle, an unseen forced wrenched him back. What felt like stone hands threw him into the air, and his body crashed painfully into the ceiling. As his body fell back down to the floor, it struck the wood and he felt several bones break. The intense pain forced the lights out, and the world became black.

When light again filled Valon's unfocused eyes, his immediate thought was that he no longer felt pain. The man sat up warily, concerned that the absence of pain was a misjudgment that would cause him to inflict more damage on his broken body. But whatever happened moments before, the young man couldn't find any evidence of it now.

Valon's eagerness to leave the house returned, awakening his limbs, and he hastily made his way to his feet. He opened the front door and halted in confusion to find nothing beyond the frame. He could see the world through the windows, still thriving in the early evening sunlight that lit the living room. But to his bewilderment, Valon saw nothing but a black, empty void when he stood at the open door.

"Stand guard, slave," a dark voice rumbled through him.

In a panic, Valon turned back to the living room to find the source of the sound, but no one stood behind him. On the floor, just five feet away, Valon saw the body of a man, his eyes and mouth open, frozen in horror. Blood pooled around the stranger's head and seeped through the exposed subfloor boards. When Valon could make his eyes remain still enough to take in the dead man's face, he realized in his panic that the stricken face was his own.

Valon couldn't remember how long he sat down on the living room sofa to stare at his lifeless body on the floor; it might have been days. Flashes of understanding came and went while the room too dissolved around him but then reappeared when something happened: the telephone rang, the postman pushed mail through the slat in the front door, or the wall clock chimed at noon.

It was all very much like a dream. The landscape of the house fell away from Valon's mind, then returned when something changed, but it never quite felt concrete. In time, he could exercise some control over his mind and shut out certain stimuli, and this allowed him to rest for longer.

Valon's head jerked sharply at the sound of three hard knocks upon the front door. Attempting to look through the living room glass to determine who was there, something pulled the man's body off the sofa with a stone's strength. Valon flew off the sofa a full ten feet towards the coat closet door. The invisible force turned him around to slam his back against the closet. It held Valon's chest, legs, and arms rigidly in position as if he were a shield. Without speaking, the young man understood that he was to stand sentry over the room and guard the door.

After a series of repeated knocks banged against the home's front door, Valon saw it crash open from his peripheral. From the void, a tall man wearing an olive uniform walk into the foyer. With both hands, the man held a gun pointed at the floor.

"County sheriff," the man called loudly. "Is anyone home?"

From the void behind the sheriff appeared Jolene

White, a young blonde holding her purse pensively in the darkened foyer. Before she could call out Valon's name, she screamed in panic at the sight of his dead body lying on the living room floor. The sheriff stopped the young woman's instinctive advance toward her boyfriend.

"No, no, miss," he whispered as his arm firmly caught the girl. "You need to leave it be. He's dead. I'm sorry, but he's gone."

Jolene buried her head into the man's chest and held onto him in panic. From his lapel, the sheriff seized his radio broach and called to confirm that he had located Valon Williams, that the man was deceased, and to request that backup and the paramedics be dispatched.

"You're all right," he said to the young woman repeatedly. "Go wait outside away from the house for me right now. You're certain no one else would be here?"

"No," Jolene's voice caught as she trembled, "he lives alone."

"Okay, go now," the sheriff told her. "Go down by my car and wait for other officers to arrive."

The girl nodded and clumsily walked backward before disappearing into the void beyond the front door.

Left alone, the sheriff pulled his gun from his holster and kept it aimed at the floor.

"Is anyone in the house?" he yelled. "Call out now, so I know you're here!"

The man paced slowly through the living room and made his way through the dining room and the kitchen. When he had started down the rear hall past the laundry and guest room, he shouted out the same order again to receive only silence. Returning through the study and landing back in the foyer, the sheriff climbed the steps to the second floor.

Valon remained affixed to the coat closet door. He

could hear the sheriff's footfalls through the timber of the home's walls. After some time searching out of sight, the sheriff returned downstairs and approached the corpse on the floor. Holstering his gun, he stared down, taking in the view of Valon William's lifeless face, which still bore a distinctive expression of terror. The sheriff averted his eyes from the face several times before he turned and looked up at the coat closet.

The man's expression startled Valon. It was as if he hadn't noticed the closet door during his first search of the downstairs. He reached again for his gun and withdrew it, pointing it downward in front of him. The sheriff approached and reached for the knob cautiously.

Valon felt the stone's grip pull his body backward through the wooden door and down to the ground until he crouched at the back of the closet under the stairs.

The door opened, and the sheriff swiftly pushed aside the coats that hung on the rack. He shone a flashlight beam toward Valon before noticing the solitary lightbulb above his head and reached to pull on the hanging cord to light the space.

In time, the sheriff seemed to relax again, and soon shut off the light. Closing the door, he shuttered Valon in the dark.

"Rest," the voice rumbled beside him and released his grip.

Finally able to move again, Valon thought to rise and leave the tight, claustrophobic space. But he remained silent and still. Taken by grief and the sense of emptiness all around him, Valon drew up his legs to his chin, closed his eyes, and cried silently into his shirtsleeve.

CHAPTER TWENTY-SEVEN

The dream shifted wildly.

Valon rose to walk out of the closet to stand in the living room. The garish light of mid-morning assaulted his eyes, but the gleam did not hurt.

He turned to see two men descending the staircase. One was Richard, Maggie's husband. Valon felt a tinge of irritation at the sight of him. The man only reminded the ghost of the intense grief he felt for Margaret.

Valon couldn't say how long she'd been gone from the house, as he had hidden from the sight of her husband. He frequented the back of the coat closet to rest, the quiet, dark space no longer instilling him with fear. Without his lover, this existence had become too terrible to bear, and he shut his eyes in exhaustion, escaping into the isolation whenever he could.

But without explanation, Valon was thoroughly awake.

"Can I get you something to drink?" Richard asked the young man who accompanied him down the staircase. "I have a nice bourbon, or I can open up some wine for us."

"That's very kind of you, sir," answered Tony, "but I

don't drink alcohol. I'll take some water if you don't mind."

"Water?" Richard asked in mock disgust. "Is that what the kids drink now? That's a damned crime. The Prohibitionists have finally been reborn, I see."

Tony laughed at the man's color. "Let's just say I drank more than my fair share when I was a kid. Now, it gets in the way of everything."

"When you were a kid?" Richard asked with an incredulous laugh. "Son, that's the point of alcohol—to get in the way of everything and let you have a break from your troubles. Christ, my mother would've loved a son like you. I'll bet you're dating a fine Christian woman with your sights on marriage and a family?"

"I would love to be a father," answered the young man.

Richard shook his head and waved to lead Tony into the kitchen, where he pulled a jug of filtered water from the refrigerator. Richard poured each of them a glassful and handed one to his incorruptible guest.

"To your disgraceful liver—clean as a whistle," toasted the man and clinked his glass against Tony's with a poorly concealed roll of his eyes. "So, tell me what you're thinking."

"Like I said, I want to do most of this on my own for a few reasons," Tony began. "For one, I need to learn what I don't know about the craft. Jefferson Construction has limited me only to the scrap jobs—those they think I'm qualified for only because more seasoned subcontractors are unavailable. I realize that's the game, that in time I'll find myself in the position to learn and do more. But, I'm ready for more now, and taking on a job like this, by myself, will mean I get to learn everything.

"Now, that might give you pause," Tony continued, "but I promise to commit to learning—to producing only the best work possible. Of course, that means I'll need time. Looking around today, I see it will take me at least two years to renovate this house by myself. I'll have to refinish almost every surface, and that's only if what's underneath doesn't need to be pulled apart and rebuilt completely. Two of the bathrooms need to be gutted; this kitchen alone will need months. This cabinetry was purchased on the cheap back in the eighties. It doesn't serve the rest of the home's design or craftsmanship at all. So, I'm not just going to restore your home, I'm going to renovate it—and the final product will look like the house was always a landmark home."

"I admire your ambition," said Richard when the boy went quiet, "but like I said before you saw it all, I don't have the money for that. You're talking, what… two, three hundred thousand dollars? Son, I'm retired, and the house isn't even paid off."

"I can do everything for under fifty grand," said Tony boldly.

"Nonsense," Richard countered. "Replacing these cabinets alone will cost that much. I know the price of things, and there's no way you could ever do what you're suggesting for fifty thousand. Your service pay alone will be half of that."

"I don't want a dime," Tony countered, "I want the opportunity to do it on my own, as I've described. I'm not interested in selecting cabinets from Lowes and ordering them for installation. I want to design the cabinets from scratch specifically for this space, build them by hand, and install them entirely by myself. I want to create pieces of art that will look so beautiful in this room, you'll never want to leave it. I'll probably need an electrician and a plumber at some point, but only to ensure we pass inspection. All I truly need are the materials to build my dream.

The price of my service is that you allow me the time I'm asking for and that you let me have the project filmed and photographed from beginning to end. I want this house to be the centerpiece of my portfolio. I want it to be the reason your neighbors will spend top dollar to have me come and resurrect their homes when I'm done."

Tony lifted the water glass to his lips and took a deep drink of the cold liquid.

"So, I could pay you as we went along? Richard asked pensively. "You wouldn't need a deposit check? Half up front and half on completion?"

"Not at all," the young man answered. "You can give me what I need to purchase from week to week. Hell, you can Venmo me the moment I hand over a receipt if that's better for you."

"I can what?" Richard scowled, perplexed. "Venbo?"

"Venmo," smiled Tony, "or use PayPal, or Apple Pay me —transfer the reimbursement through your phone. You can write a check or give me cash, of course, if you prefer."

"Oh, okay," Richard nodded. "My daughter was telling me about that, but she let me get away with avoiding it when I played dumb. Perhaps, I'll let you show me how telephone money happens?"

"You got it," Tony beamed.

"When are you thinking about doing this?" the man asked.

"I'm ready to start when you are," Tony shrugged his broad shoulders. "I could start tomorrow if you're down."

Richard fell silent and appeared to ponder the offer, his eyes wandering around the room.

"Why don't you give me a couple of days to think about it?" said Richard. "I want to discuss your offer with some friends."

"Sure, that sounds fine," Tony answered enthusiastically.

He reached into the front pocket of his charcoal denim pants and pulled out his cellphone contained within a black plastic case. Using his thumb, Tony opened a hidden door in the back of the case to reveal a storage slot meant to act as a thin wallet. Richard saw it contained two credit cards. From behind them, Tony pulled out a business card and handed it to the man. The unadorned white vellum had Tony's name embossed in a clean sans-serif font with his title and phone number listed beneath. His title read: Artisan.

"Anthony De Luca," read Richard as he held the card at a distance to see it properly. "That must be an Italian name? Son of Luke?"

"Fourth generation American," Tony answered. "I'm told we came from Naples at the start of the twentieth century."

"Your parents live around here?" asked Richard.

"I grew up in Oxnard," he clarified. "The family started out in New York, and many are still there, but my grandparents moved to Los Angeles in the fifties, and we've been in California ever since."

"My wife was born in L.A.," said Richard, "and she moved to San Diego with me when we got married—we raised our daughter there. Forgive me—Margaret, my wife, passed away last year from cancer. I don't think I mentioned that."

"Oh, I'm very sorry," said Tony, his smile darkening.

"Thank you, son," Richard nodded. "We came up here after I retired about five years ago. Cambria was always our favorite little place on the coast, and I'm glad she could be here for at least a little while before the disease took her. What drew you here?"

"I live over in Los Osos, but the whole coastal region drew me because of the opportunities to start my career. It might seem rural country to the folks from San Francisco or Los Angeles, or San Diego," he gestured at Richard, "but there are a lot of very wealthy homes between Pismo and Monterey. Most of those owners have the pockets to invest in artistans to build the very best for them."

"Is that how you see yourself," asked Richard, "an artist?"

"Absolutely," Tony answered. "At least, that's what I mean to become. I'm not interested in small pieces or even a specific craft, but homes as a whole. I want to take the bones of an architect's design and bring it to life in a way a blueprint simply can't realize.

"I saw your house several times before I drummed up the nerve to approach you," Tony continued. "I don't mean this as a slight—I realize now you've only been here a short time. I could see the house hadn't been taken care of like she deserves — it's what drew me to her. The original builder seems to have envisioned something beautiful, but there were too many corners cut: the thin railing of the front porch, the plain window cases on the second floor, or even the door frame, which is too crudely cut to hold such a remarkable, ornate front door. They might not have seemed like a big deal at the time, but compromises can quickly add up and fail the vision of a house like this. Seeing the inside only strengthens my point. The living and dining rooms are excellent, their construction inspiring even, but then I find myself sitting in a basic kitchen that doesn't fit the craftsman style of the rest of the house."

"I'm happy you see all of that," Richard said, "and I don't resent your telling me. I thought it was a beautiful house when I saw it, particularly from the curb, but I could also see I had my work cut out for me if I were to live another twenty years here.

"Margaret insisted on the house because she loved its character and location. I told her we didn't need a house this large for retirement, and I had no interest in remodeling anything when we would rather travel and enjoy each other. But I caved in the end and let her have her way.

Richard lifted his glass to take another sip of water.

"That's how every story about a successful marriage concludes, if you're serious about taking one on," Richard winked.

"I'll keep that in mind." Tony lifted his water glass in deference before taking a large gulp to finish it off. "Well, I don't want to take up any more of your time."

"Very good then," said Richard, and he rose from his seat to walk the young man out. "You've given me a lot to think about, and I promise not to keep you waiting too long for my decision."

"I really appreciate the opportunity," said Tony, and he reached for Richard's hand when they arrived at the front door. "Thank you for your consideration, sir,"

With an honest, gleaming smile, Tony turned and walked through the front door into the void.

Valon could tell the young man's offer had thrilled Richard.

"Peril," the voice whispered.

The voice rang loudly in Valon's head. The ghost did not respond but watched Richard return through the house to the kitchen. There, the man pulled a bottle of wine and opened it noisily with an electric corkscrew.

"Peril," the whisper came again, its deep, animalistic growl resonating in Valon's mind to occlude all other sounds.

Richard pulled a stemmed glass from a cupboard and poured himself a generous serving of the wine. He gave hardly any time for the deep red fluid to settle in the glass before whisking it away upstairs.

"Impede this danger to my rest," the voice rumbled its whisper.

Valon didn't respond, more from uncertainty than a desire to defy the voice. At once, Valon's body was seized painfully and pushed up the stairs and through the upper hallway to the master bedroom.

"Destroy him," rumbled the voice, filled with malice that terrified Valon.

"Why do you say this to me?" Valon coughed when the grip over his body released and allowed him to breathe.

"Destroy this threat to my rest," whispered the voice. "Kill him."

"No," insisted Valon with a wounded cry, "I will not harm Richard."

A pain seized him, unlike anything the young man had ever thought possible. The room around Valon disappeared as the light of the world darkened to pitch black. Valon could hear nothing, see nothing, but felt a white-hot pain invade his every thought. It seared through his mind for what seemed like seconds or minutes or days or weeks. Time did not exist in this void. All that was present was Valon's agony—pain without end.

When the last fragments of his remaining consciousness were in danger of deserting him, Valon heard the voice whisper to him again.

"If I must rise from my rest to slay a mortal, I will leave you here and replace you with another," said the voice, the deep rumble articulating his words silently through the growl of an angry beast.

"Slave…" the voice echoed with disgust.

Yes, Master, Valon's feeble thoughts cried.

The pain stopped, disappearing from the young man's mind as if it had never happened. The house returned all around him. The light of day poured through the windows flooded into Valon's unmasked eyes, terrifying him. His body trembled wildly, and his breath came in uneven pants. Valon attempted to take a step forward, but his legs gave out, and he stumbled forward, reaching for anything to stop his fall.

Focus, he thought, and in time he could stand up again. Valon made his way through the bedroom to the open door of the bathroom, where Richard was bent over the large clawed bathtub. He closed the tap and stood up again, reaching to unbutton his white shirt.

Turning back, Richard's body seized up as he looked toward Valon. The ghost's fear had contracted the molecules of its substance together, and Richard could see him plainly as he stood there.

"What are you doing here, son?" Richard calmly asked the stranger. "This is my home."

The man's voice overwhelmed Valon. Richard spoke not with anger but kindly. His voice bore concern for Valon in a manner that Maggie always insisted was why she trusted the man. Indeed, Valon could see plainly that, regardless of Richard's fear, he wanted to be kind and helpful, if he could.

"You should leave, now," said Richard, again calmly, "there's nothing for you here. Do you need assistance?"

Valon wanted to tell the man how sorry he was, say to Richard how he must leave the house to find safety, but no sound came from his voice. Valon realized for the first time that he couldn't make a sound in front of this man. His throat closed around the words before he could deliver them.

Valon thought to turn away. He pivoted on his foot as if he would leave, but he immediately felt the pain threaten to return. Fear seizing hold of him again, Valon looked to Richard and pushed him backward with a violent blast, the blow from his mind causing the man to land against the floor, his head slamming against the bathtub on the way down.

Richard twitched as his limbs came to rest, his central nervous system attempting to reassemble the maligned torso in vain. The man was dying. The light in Ricard's eyes rapidly faded away, and soon he was gone.

Valon entered the bathroom and fell to his knees painfully—the agony of what he'd done defeated him. He wept by Richard's body, sitting back against the vanity cabinetry to pull his knees to his chest.

What had he done? He had betrayed Maggie; failed to protect her husband as she'd begged him to with her final words. And there the man lay, his face a mask of fear, frozen in death.

Valon tried in vain to close the man's eyes, but he could do nothing now; the exertion of his villainy had rendered him too weak to affect the change. The ghost rose to his knees when he couldn't bear to sit beside the body anymore, holding onto the vanity for support.

At last standing, Valon looked into the mirror and realized he could see his reflection, something that had rarely happened before. He looked deep into his own eyes, seeing the steel blue color of his irises shining back at him.

Terror seized him again, and he trembled as if from what he saw in the glass.

"Wake up, Kristen!" he screamed.

CHAPTER TWENTY-EIGHT

Tony didn't open his eyes when he heard glass shatter from far away. He still held firmly onto the sweet comfort of sleep. When heard Penny barking, some part of Tony's mind recognized he needed to return to consciousness, but rest still held onto him. It was eventually the loud crash of wood being ripped to pieces that forced his eyes open.

Tony first noticed how the wall lamps in the guest room we turned on. The flood of amber light pursued him even when he closed his eyelids again in protest. Resting chest down upon the air mattress, the young man faced just right of the bed. He could hear a quiet scratching sound, and again he forced his eyes open to allow the room's unmasked electric light in through his retinas.

A simple logic supported Tony's presumption: if the lights were on, Kristen must be awake, and he should get up. But his limbs felt like iron weights—he had rarely slept so hard. Perhaps there was something more to say about this air mattress that held him. Maybe it was the three rounds of sex that had done him in.

And then he smelled it.

A putrid odor filled Tony's nostrils, causing him to scrunch his nose and bring his hand to his face. Burning garbage or rotten eggs, or maybe even sulfur —the sharp, offensive smell burned his throat and eyes.

"What is that?" he moaned, control returning to his limbs as he awoke. "Kristen?"

Turning over in the bed to face her, Tony found Kristen lying beside him naked. Her eyes were closed as if she were still asleep. On her chest lay the Ouija board just under her chin. In her right hand was the indicator piece, which she slid in small increments over the letters, moving and then stopping in a slow rhythm, creating a low scratching.

"Kristen," he said, baffled by the sight, then moved to sit up in bed beside her.

Tony nudged her gently. He didn't care about the Ouija board but wanted her to stop playing with it and account for the terrible smell. The synapses of his mind were still landing incorrectly, and he double-checked his senses a few times to prove to himself what he smelled and saw were real.

"Kristen," he raised his voice and reached to lift her hand from the small heart-shaped piece of plastic.

With the woman's hand in his own, Tony realized the indicator piece was still sliding across the board, one little movement at a time. It stopped and started every two seconds again, stopping over the next letter of the alphabet, arranged in sequence along two rows.

His only thought was that it must be a toy with magnets affixed underneath to slide the indicator back and forth. The makers programmed it to entertain partygoers with spooky words, no doubt. Tony reached with his other hand to stop and lift the piece from the board, but found that it was not movable—whatever held it in place was stronger than small magnets.

From outside the guest room, Tony heard a clamoring of wood creaking. It sounded as if something enormous were moving along the floor from the living room through the foyer and library. When the sound reached the entrance to the hallway where the guest room lay, Tony swung his legs to the floor in search of his clothes.

"Hello?!" his voice shot loudly at whoever approached. The naked man found the denim pants where he'd cast them near the foot of the mattress, but not his briefs.

From atop the Ouija board on Kristen's chest, Tony saw the indicator fly violently toward the window, shattering the glass. The hairs on his neck and arm prickled painfully. Tony pulled on his denim work pants, commando-style, and struggled to push the fat metal hardware through the stiff material's buttonholes.

On both sides of the room, the bulbs in the glass wall lamps popped loudly, leaving the room in the same darkness of the hallway outside the open door.

The change confounded Tony. He'd never experienced a moment in his life where he'd felt so helpless, so alone, and Tony suffered a breed of fear that astounded him as it froze his legs.

From the hallway, Tony heard whatever approached arrive at the door frame. The young man could not see what it was, even in the dim moonlight that poured through the broken window. But Tony could feel its presence through his other senses. The smell intensified, burning his eyes as if whatever stood in the doorframe exhaled the rancid odor. The sound in the room changed. It dampened, muffling even the noise of Tony's breathing. His ears closed to guard him against an attack.

Tony thought to turn on his iPhone and engage the

flashlight, but his feeble attempts to search in his pockets resulted in nothing. A glance down at the pitch-black floor quickly proved futile.

"Answer me!" Tony's voice yelled as he pushed through his fear, standing as large as his chest would allow for, the deep timbre of his baritone booming in his closed ears more strongly than he expected. "Who the fuck is there?!"

From behind his head, Tony heard whispering, a low din of syllables and phrases he couldn't make out. When he turned his head sharply, he found the location of the voices immediately changed. This unnerving strategy of the silent language moving behind him whenever he turned soon crescendoed Tony's dread at the damning realization they didn't come from behind him. The voices were inside his head.

Tony saw a flash of light, almost imperceptible to his eyes, and then another. It seemed like a trick, the ghost image of something in his field of vision that lingered on his retinas just barely long enough to make out a figure. He moved his eyes, trying to see the image better, but nothing seemed to improve his clarity of vision. Slowly, the flashes increased, and Tony saw more.

And then the pain started.

He felt sick—his chest constricted and became paralyzed as if he couldn't breathe. Behind Tony's eyes grew such sharp discomfort that he lost his fear of the moment and thought to run from the room and locate fresh air. He would grab Kristen from off the mattress and carry her out of the room, then make his way to the backyard. But then Tony realized he couldn't control any part of his body. As his center of gravity began to spin, Tony expected to feel his body hit the mattress or floor when he fell to the ground. But he felt nothing, and after a few more seconds, his consciousness abandoned him altogether. His last thought was of the face that burned in his mind.

THE SOUND of a woman's scream opened Tony's eyes with a violent start. He didn't understand where he was or what the noise was, other than it was the piercing shriek of a woman's voice.

"Tony! TONY!" the voice screamed in an absolute panic.

He felt adrenaline shoot into his bloodstream, and his heart pumped dangerously fast. In less than a second, he regained control of his limbs and shot up. Though Tony was in the dark, the lights from the hallway lit up the guest room well enough that he could orient himself.

"Tony!" the voice cried a third time.

It was Kristen's voice, he realized, and he shot up out of bed, unaware that he wore only his jeans. He raced barefoot into the hallway, shaking off the bright contrast of the lamps but followed the light toward the library, around the foyer and staircase until he pounded into the living room.

Tony narrowly avoided colliding with Kristen, who crouched on the floor in front of what appeared to be a small explosion of broken glass and wood. Regaining his footing upon the debris, he took in the sight without thinking to first respond to her screams.

The coat closet door was wide open. The iron handle appeared stuck into the wall as if someone had opened it with such force that it buried into the oak paneling like an arrowhead. They had broken off the lower slats of the door—its pieces lay scattered about the room. There were slivers of cracked glass among them. Tony thought they had come from the closet lightbulb, now gone from its socket. But they had also left shattered glass along the living room and dining room in a trail leading to the kitchen. From his vantage, Tony could see they had shattered the rear glass door, opening the kitchen to the backyard.

Kristen's hands bore streaks of blood, and she struggled to keep from touching her face to muffle her deep, wailing sobs. At her knees, where the woman had fallen to the ground, lay Penny's lifeless body. The Husky's silver and white head was stained with blood.

THE END

THE GHOST OF CAMBRIA TRILOGY

THE STORY CONCLUDES

BOOK #3: What if the person you fear the most is the one who has kept you safe from real danger?

Every night, Kristen Cole is visited by a stranger who appears in her dreams with startling clarity. There is no doubt left in her mind: the man with his brooding brow and adoring steel-blue eyes is a ghost. And Kristen now knows his name: Valon William. He has shared his mind with the mistress of his house and the memories of the home's previous occupants. But Valon has also shown Kristen his rage and his intolerance for her corporeal suitors.

Waking early this morning, Kristen found her lover safely asleep by her side. She set aside her fears of Tony De Luca falling victim to the jealous designs of the unseen occupant of her home. But rising from bed, Kristen found her silver and white Husky lying lifeless on the floor, the dog's muzzle stained with blood. Wrought with vengeful anger, Kristen decides she will burn the house to the ground.

What started as an erotic dream, quickly became a seduction. What turned into a nightmare, has become a fight for Kristen Cole's life.

ABOUT THE AUTHOR

Joseph Stone is a historical and dark fantasy novelist who lives in San Diego, California. He holds a Bachelor of Science in Psychology from San Diego State University and a Master of Arts in Industrial and Organizational Psychology from The Chicago School of Professional Psychology.

To learn of upcoming releases, visit:

www.AuthorJosephStone.com

Follow Stone at:

- amazon.com/author/josephstone
- goodreads.com/joseph_stone
- instagram.com/josephstoneauthor
- facebook.com/josephstoneauthor
- twitter.com/authorjoestone